Beware the Nothing Much

by
E.R. Turner

Copyright © 1998 by Ella Ruth Bergera

ALL RIGHTS RESERVED.

No part of this book may be reproduced in any form whatsoever, whether by graphic, visual, electronic, filming, microfilming, tape recording, or any other means, without written permission of the author, except in the case of brief passages embodied in critical reviews and articles where the ISBN and author are mentioned.

This book is a work of fiction. All characters and events are the work of the author's imagination and any resemblance to real people or events is coincidental.

GRANITE
PUBLISHING & DISTRIBUTION

Distributed by:
Granite Publishing and Distribution, L.L.C.
270 S. Mountainlands Dr Suite 7 • Orem, UT 84058
(801) 229-9023 • Toll Free (800) 574-5779
FAX (801) 229-1924

Additional Works by E.R. Turner...

The Reunion; Generations of Marsh family members learn the true meaning of "As I have loved you, love one another."

To Seek a Bird's Nest; The four Elizabeths, each seeking the peace that passeth all understanding, must meet the problems of her time with wisdom and fortitude.

ISBN: 1-57636-053-9
Library of Congress Catalog Card Number: 98-85006
Production by: *SunRise Publishing, Orem, Utah 1-888-732-2470*

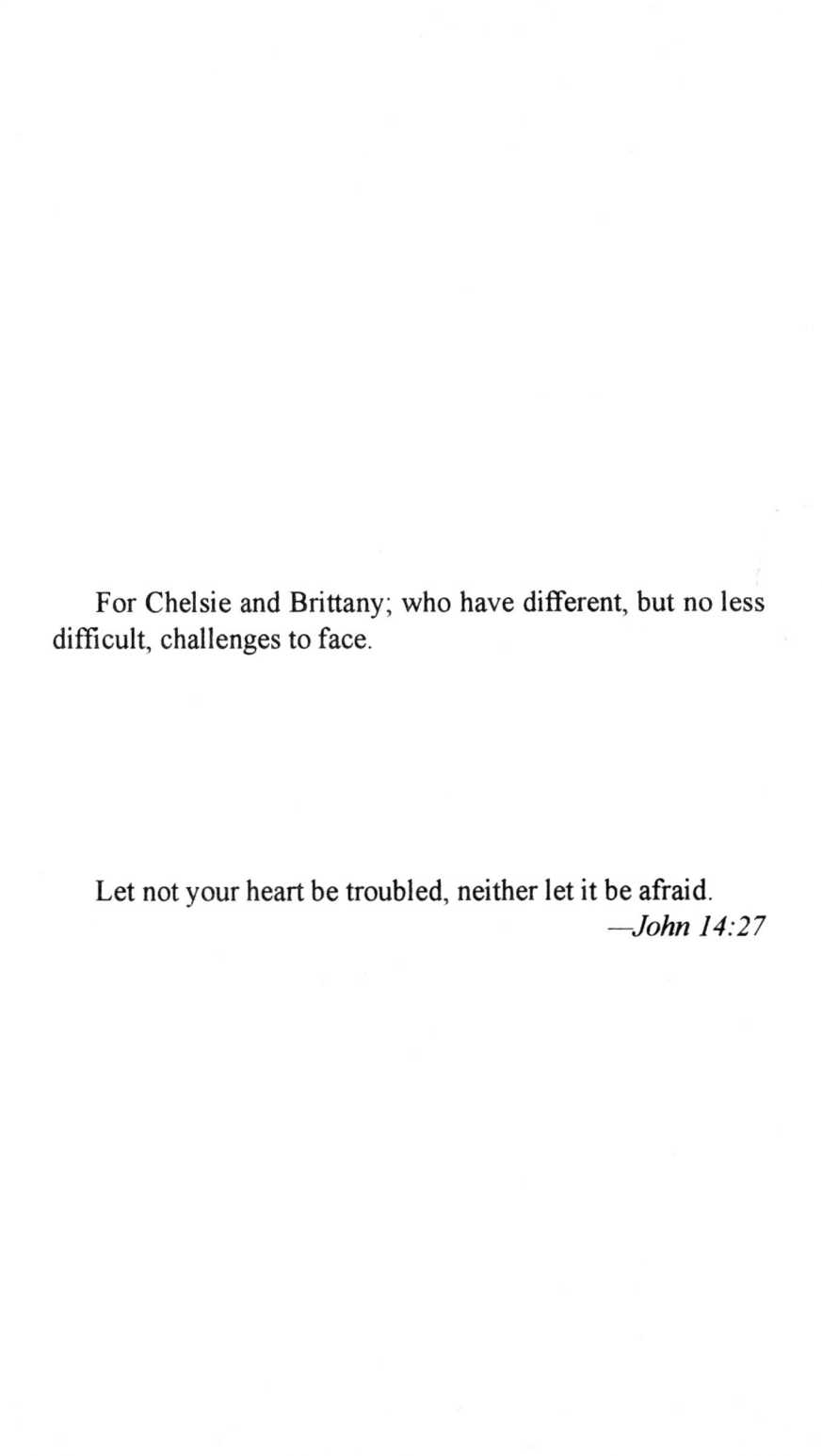

For Chelsie and Brittany; who have different, but no less difficult, challenges to face.

Let not your heart be troubled, neither let it be afraid.
—*John 14:27*

Chapter One

Emma. Such a plain, ordinary name, I thought. Just about as plain and ordinary as me. Looking in the mirror again I couldn't find one redeeming feature. Dishwater blond (ugh—but what else could it be called?) hair without a sign of curl or wave, and a sprinkle of hated freckles across a very ordinary nose. Lips as plain as my name. And my eyes? Well, they are my only good feature—gold-flecked hazel fringed with long, curly lashes. But even they can't offset my otherwise bland face. There's nothing about me that is worth looking at twice. Sure, mama always says a person's character is what really counts. And Aunt Betsy predicts that my baby fat will be gone soon.

But if looks aren't all that important, how come people are always saying how cute Ivy is? She doesn't have any baby fat. And her wavy auburn hair gleams when the sun is at her back. True, her brown eyes are set closer together than she likes, but her smooth, straight nose looks great above her full pink lips.

It just isn't fair! Even her name is special. Just three letters but they bring to mind the plant that grows so free, reaching out wherever it wants to go. Maybe that's why Ivy always seems to get whatever she wants. She gets to stay out later at night than I do and she doesn't have to explain where she's going every time she leaves the house.

I can't go anywhere without telling mama first. And I know better than to ask to stay out later than nine o'clock ANY night, whether it's the Monday night movie or somebody's birthday party.

Ivy and I are best friends, but I figured out long ago that it's because she knows that with me there will never be any competition in the things that matter to her. Things like looks, clothes, and boys. Sure, I get better grades in school, but she doesn't think all that stuff they teach us is very important anyway. "What's the point," she often says, "when we're just going to grow up and get married and never use any of this stuff?"

You may wonder what kind of relationship ours could be. Well, I'll tell you. I know that if I don't hold on to my fragile best friend position with Ivy, I won't have any best friend at all. And that's a powerful motivator when you're twelve years old, homely, and there aren't that many other 'acceptable' kids your age in town.

You have to understand how it is in small towns like ours. You could have a best friend who's your friend at her convenience, or you could have no best friend at all. I settled years ago for the convenient friend. It wouldn't be so bad if I lived in a bigger town where there are more friends to choose from. But living here in Grassville doesn't leave many choices.

There were less than a dozen kids in our sixth grade this past year, some of whom live across the creek in what we call 'tag town,' so you can't count them. Kids there move in and out whenever their folks move on looking for work elsewhere. Most of those families follow the crop seasons, but each year a few families stay through the year, the luckier dads working at the sawmill while others take any odd jobs they can get in town or on the few surrounding farms. The 'tag town' kids know we think we're better than them and they stay to themselves. True, we have to go to school together, but we don't have to play with each other or hang around together after school.

Mama has been to some of their sorry little shacks helping with sickness, or sharing fresh-baked bread or bottled fruit. I heard her tell daddy one night that the husband of one of the sick women quietly said that even though mama didn't recognize him, he remembered her. She had given him some food and what few pennies she had five years earlier, during the worst of the Depression when he was crossing the country looking for work. Mama said he smiled as he asked, "You didn't know that your house was marked as a place where a hungry man could get food, did you?"

There had been rumors to that effect, but we hadn't known if they were true. At any rate, mama asked me once why I didn't bring that nice little Mary Ruiz home to play sometime. I just mumbled something about her having to stay home and help with her little brothers and sister. I knew mama would never approve that I couldn't afford to lose face with the few friends I did have if I acted friendly with any of those 'tag town' kids.

You have to understand about my mama. She's not like Ivy's mother and most of the other women in Grassville. She doesn't meet at the store every afternoon to gossip.

"Isn't it just awful the way that Denton woman wears those tight dresses and that bright red lipstick!"

"And did you hear about Sally Oliver flirting with anybody in long pants? Honestly! Even if she is simple-minded, she's nothing but trash."

"And what about that awful drunkard of a brother of hers! It's amazing that the single teachers are still willing to board with Mrs. Oliver!"

They look down their noses, too, at the 'tag town' women who come to the store trying to make their few pennies stretch as far as possible.

When mama was invited to join their newly-formed Grassville Ladies Hospitality Club, I heard her tell daddy that the ladies never seemed to find time to be hospitable to any of the poor women in 'tag town.' They were always too busy trying to keep the riff-raff out of Grassville proper. Once when a house in town came up vacant, a family from across the creek went to look at it. In no time at all, the Ladies Hospitality rallied together and found someone "more suitable" to move into it. After that, mama wasn't interested in being in their elect little club.

I tried to get her to join, stretching the truth a mile about what nice things those ladies were always doing for other people. But it didn't do any good. Truth be known, I didn't like most of those ladies much myself, but mama, by not being one of them, just gave Ivy more ammunition to use against me. She was always talking about how her mama had been the president since the beginning and what a wonderful job she was doing.

In a couple more weeks school will start and I am glad. I like reading and spelling and history and arithmetic and am good at them. I'm not too crazy about science and penmanship, but I do think geography is fun, especially when we learn about other countries. In fact, my secret dream is to travel all around the world some day. But I've got sense enough never to talk about that with Ivy. Once, awhile back, I mentioned something about how great it would be to travel.

She laughed her head off and said, "You!? With all your family all crowded together in your dinky little house! Hah! You'll never have enough money to go as far as Salt Lake, let alone out of the country! Why would you want to travel anyway? Everything a person could want is right here in Grassville."

I knew her only dream was getting out of school and

marrying Robbie Banks. She had been crazy about him since first grade.

But I want more than that out of life. So I kept my mouth shut and just let her think that Grassville was enough for me, too.

And it is for now. Grassville is a great place to live. Most of the houses are situated between the creek and the railroad tracks. Right in the middle of town is Main Street with a General Store that sells everything from clothes to food. There's a Confectionery next door where we can buy double-decker ice cream cones for a nickel. On the other side of the store is the moving picture theater that's open every Monday night from seven to nine for a movie and a Buck Rogers or Flash Gordon serial.

Two blocks east of Main Street is our two-story schoolhouse. It's for first through ninth grades. The high school kids have to ride the bus to Sommerset, the county seat twenty-five miles south.

The doctor's office is on the block between Main and the school. It's a big, old frame house. Dr. Louganis and his wife, who's a nurse, live upstairs. The downstairs is divided into a waiting room, examination room, and simple operating room where I had my tonsils out last year.

But, most important, there are mountains on the north and west sides of town where I like to climb to look out at the world beyond Grassville and dream of seeing it all someday.

The two new teachers would be moving into Mrs. Oliver's boarding house any day now. She has room for five teachers and, since there are three holdovers from last year, us kids have all been hoping to be there when the new teachers move in. The married teachers live in town so we already know who they are. I know who all my seventh grade teachers will be except for English, since the old English teacher moved away when school ended last spring. I don't have to take science this year so I'm not too interested in that teacher.

"Look, there's the peddler's truck stopping over at Oliver's." Ivy and I were sitting on her front porch. Her house is kittycorner across the street. We'd been waiting there since noon to see if the new teachers would arrive today.

But only one man got out of the passenger side of the truck and lifted a suitcase and two boxes out of the back.

"Well, that makes two men teachers there now," Ivy commented. "I wonder if the other new teacher will be a man, too."

We kept watching as the truck drove away and the man carried his things into the house. He seemed sorta nondescript and colorless and I hoped he wasn't the new English teacher.

Next morning Ivy filled me in on all the details. "He's Mr. Lewis from Idaho and has taught junior high science for four years. He was at an institute this summer where he met our old science teacher. That's how he found out about the opening here." She added disgustedly, "He's not married and doesn't even have a girl friend."

I didn't need to ask her how she knew all this. With a mother like hers, no information is private for very long in this town. And I knew that the report was accurate. Mrs. Greeley was nothing, if not persistent, in her search for gossip.

So now there was nothing to do but wait for the last teacher to arrive. And when she did, it was so unobtrusive and quick no one in town was on hand to watch.

We found out later that she came in on the Stage, a combination bus and delivery vehicle that comes to town from Sommerset twice a week. She hadn't come on Wednesday when we were all standing around watching for the Stage but, instead, arrived Sunday evening just about the time everybody in town was sitting down to supper.

Talk was she only had two suitcases and quickly disappeared into her room at Oliver's. Mrs. Oliver reported later that she stopped just long enough to introduce herself to the other teachers seated at the table and said, no thanks, she wasn't hungry, she'd just go unpack and get ready for school tomorrow.

Well, I can tell you, the whole town couldn't wait for school to start. And Ivy's mama was madder than a wet hen when she discovered that she wouldn't be the first one to know about the new teacher. I was happy as could be when Ivy told me that even though her mama had got up at the crack of dawn on Monday to watch for her, she had already gone to school and was busy getting her room ready.

The first day of school went fairly well, all things considered. Our classes went about as smooth as expected, with the same kids throwing spitballs and erasers this year as last.

When it was time for our English class, the anticipation was almost unbearable. After some jockeying for desks, we each settled down and watched expectantly for the teacher to come in.

Just as the bell rang for class to start, in walked the most strikingly beautiful person I've ever seen. Her glossy raven hair was tucked securely into a chignon at the back of her neck highlighting her delicate, beautiful face. Her eyes, which stopped all talking dead still as she looked at each one of us in turn, were the loveliest green, matching perfectly her simple green dress. When her lips broke into a smile, I felt like dropping to my knees in adoration. It wasn't just me. Every person in class sat spellbound, none of us daring to take our eyes off this wonderful apparition in case she disappeared. The room was filled with enchantment.

"Good morning, class. I'm Miss Freeman. I hope to get to know each of you very well and that we'll enjoy this year together." With a glint of humor in her eyes she continued,

"I'm sure some of you have questions so I'll take just a few minutes now to tell you about me and then we can get on with our work."

She paused, as though thinking her words through very carefully, then asked, "Have any of you read *Heidi*?"

Two or three hands struggled reluctantly up, mine among them. Most parents in our town don't put much stock in wasting time reading. But my mama likes to read as much as I do and always makes sure I receive at least one book for Christmas or my birthday. We have no library, either in town or in school, so for those few of us who love to read, books are both treasures and well kept secrets.

"Well," Miss Freeman continued, "I hope you'll all get a chance to read *Heidi* some time. Anyway, I come from a little town in the mountains much like Heidi's home with her grandfather. I grew up loving to climb those mountains and learned a good deal about the world from being in them looking out over the valleys below. My mountains aren't as high as Heidi's, but they are high enough for pine trees on the upper levels and quaking aspens and sumacs winding their way down the slopes. Our town is a little ranching community in a neighboring state."

As she paused, I was sure I could see the area as clearly as if I were there myself.

"After I graduated from high school I moved here to Utah and received my teaching certificate. I was teaching in another part of the state when I heard about this opening. I thought I might enjoy coming here and sharing my love of English and literature with you."

None of us realized at the time but, while seeming to tell us everything about herself, Miss Freeman didn't tell us anything really personal at all. But as I listened to her gentle voice fill our room and our hearts, I didn't realize how much our lives would change in the months to come.

The routine of school, chores, play and study took on their usual pattern. Even though I was a year older, I still had to be home by nine every night. And my envy of Ivy grew as she continued to stay out late and didn't have to ask permission every time she left the house.

One day, in an unguarded moment, Ivy told me how mad her mother was that she hadn't found out anything more about Miss Freeman than everybody else knew.

"Mama invited her to join the Ladies Hospitality, but Miss Freeman just smiled and said something about waiting until she sees how things are going at school first. Mama can't understand that at all cause both Miss Conley and Miss Stewart, who live at Oliver's too, are members."

Ivy laughed, "And mama's pleased as punch that they don't know any more about Miss Freeman than she does. Mama mentioned to daddy that she might invite Miss Freeman to Sunday dinner. I was watching and when she saw daddy's smile, she hurried and changed her mind and said that if Miss Freeman is too snooty to join the Ladies Hospitality, she doesn't need to think decent people in town are going to invite her to dinner."

I was glad to hear Mrs. Greeley hadn't been able to talk Miss Freeman into joining her club. And I was glad, too, she wasn't able to stick her nose into Miss Freeman's private affairs. Nosy old busybody.

Slowly the curiosity about Miss Freeman cooled down. She was always at school before any of the other teachers and always the last to leave. Word was that the only time anybody at Mrs. Oliver's saw her was at supper and, even then, she always slipped into her chair just as the meal started and always left the table before dessert was served. She told the others she was watching her weight but no one thought she needed to worry about that one little bit.

According to the other teachers there, she even spent most of the weekend in her room or at school, claiming to be checking papers or making lesson plans.

In church on Sunday Miss Freeman was pleasant and gracious to everyone but she never stayed around afterward to visit like the rest of the people did.

"They really ought to quit trying to mind that woman's business," mama said in exasperation one Sunday coming home from church. "If she wants the town to know all about her, she'll tell them."

Daddy replied, "Well Livvy, you can't blame people

being curious about her. She keeps to herself all the time and never says one thing about her family or anything. She doesn't even go to the dances or movies. That seems kinda strange for a pretty woman like her."

"I don't care," mama shot back. "She's an excellent teacher, doesn't bother anybody, and what she does on her own time is her own concern. It's high time people mind their own business and leave hers alone!"

And as the weeks passed, gradually they did. With fall in the air, people got busy preparing for winter and stopped verbally wondering so much about Miss Freeman. And at school most of us kids in her classes, for the first time in our lives, began to openly enjoy reading.

Chapter Two

"No thanks. I don't feel like dancing right now." I walked over by the gym door and stood looking down the stairs. How can Jerry even think I'd dance with him! Doesn't he understand that I'll die of embarrassment if I try to go around the floor with someone as clumsy as him while everybody watches and laughs? I wish he'd just go away and leave me alone.

Looking back toward the dancers, I was appalled to see Ivy laughing as she danced with Jerry like she was enjoying every minute of it. How can she do that? He's so dumb and awkward I'm mortified when he even asks me to dance. I just couldn't believe that Ivy could act like she's enjoying herself.

It's not as though she likes him. She says even worse things about him than I do. Yet it doesn't seem to bother her at all to get out on the floor and dance with him and pretend she's having the time of her life. I'll never figure it out.

If Jerry lived in 'tag town' no one would have to pretend to be nice to him. But he doesn't. He came to live with his aunt and uncle after his parents didn't want him around anymore, Ivy had told me. His aunt and uncle try to make him be like the other kids in town, but it's no use. Jerry always acts dumb or hangs around where he isn't wanted. All the kids make fun of him.

Last summer, soon after he moved here, he came over to our place a few times. Sometimes my mom or brothers came out and talked to him. I tried to ignore him but he didn't seem to notice. One day when I was hanging out the washing, he came out by the clotheslines and stood around trying to talk to me.

I finally yelled, "Go on home and leave me alone Jerry Harris! Just go on home!"

"You can make me get off your property," he retorted, "but you can't make me go home!"

Oh, how I hate that stupid, dumb kid! And it seems like the worse I treat him, the more he hangs around. I just can't understand it. I certainly don't go where I'm not wanted so I can't figure out why Jerry still comes around.

Mama encourages me to be nice to him. She's tried to convince me that he's lonely and wants a friend. I know better than to argue with her, but I figure if he wants a friend, he ought to go find one somewhere else. And he ought to know by now that I'm never going to be his friend OR dance with him.

"Come on Emma, it's time to go home. Daddy and the boys want to leave early in the morning."

I took one last envious look at Ivy still whirling away and turned to leave with mama. I know I should be grateful I was even allowed to go to the Deer Hunt Dance at all, but right now I'm not much into gratitude. I'm into anger and perplexity.

"I can't believe daddy invited Jerry to go hunting with them. I know Don and Ted don't care cause they're both in high school. But I thought for sure Bruce would put a stop to it!" He's in ninth grade so he knows how us seventh graders feel about Jerry.

Mama looked at me with unconcealed disgust. "Why should Bruce put a stop to it? He knows it's not hurting anyone to have Jerry along." She paused. "You know, he's never been deer hunting and he's so happy to be included in the excitement. And," she continued, "why do you care anyway? You're not going along, so why are you making such a fuss?"

"It's just the idea of him tagging along. Now the other kids will think our family likes Jerry."

"Well, we do like him. And if you have a problem with that young lady, you need to take a good hard look at yourself. It seems to me you're blowing this whole thing way out of proportion."

I hate to admit it—and won't out loud—but mama is probably right. Just because daddy and my brothers are taking Jerry deer hunting with them doesn't mean I have to be involved.

The deer hunt is such a big deal anyway! You'd think it's

the most important thing in the world the way all the men and boys parade around in their red shirts and hats. I know we need the meat, but I still think it's dumb that everybody in town makes such a celebration of it. We even get out of school for two days! It seems to me there are lots better things to dismiss school for than riding horses up into the mountains to shoot deer.

However, I am smart enough to keep these thoughts to myself. Expressing them aloud would be blasphemy in Grassville. Or in the whole county for that matter.

Also, part of my discontent has to do with the fact that the days the hunters are gone are what mama considers ideal days to do fall housecleaning. It's not fair that just because I'm the only girl in the family, and the youngest child at that, while the boys get out of school to hunt, I have to help wash windows, stretch curtains, scrub and wax floors and dust every corner of the house. Some things in life are a real pain in the neck.

In all honesty, the work didn't take that long. I still had time to finish reading the Nancy Drew book my cousin had loaned me. How I envy Nancy her cute clothes, neat roadster and freedom to have all those adventures. I know I could solve mysteries and face down villains without fear or help just like her if I'd only get half a chance.

On Saturday afternoon, when the hunters rode back into the yard with two deer, I had to admit that even I got involved in the excitement. Maybe that's why I was so caught off guard a few minutes later when Jerry was sorting his stuff out from the rest of the things that had been taken on the hunt.

I was watching daddy and the boys take care of the horses and hang up the deer in the woodshed, when out of the corner of my eye I saw something drop out of Jerry's pack. Without thinking, I leaned over and picked it up just as he made a grab for it. I couldn't believe my eyes. It was the book *Call of The Wild*. My mouth opened in total surprise while he grabbed the book out of my hand and slid it quickly out of sight.

It was a minute before I could speak. "What are you doing with that book?"

"What do people usually do with books? I'm reading it," he muttered.

"Come on," I challenged. "Whose book is it really?"

"It's mine. Aunt Emily gave it to me for my birthday. This is my third time through it." He looked steadily at me. "What's the matter? Didn't you think I could read?"

"Sure, I know you can read. You wouldn't be in our English class if you couldn't. But I didn't think you read anything that wasn't required. Next thing you'll tell me you actually like to read," I added sarcastically.

"Well I hate to disappoint you, but I read every book I can get my hands on. Just because you think I'm dumb doesn't make me a liar. I DO like to read." Then he added quietly, "Now you can go tell all the other kids so they'll have something else to laugh at about me."

And that was what I fully intended to do—tell the other kids about Jerry and books.

But, somehow, I found myself putting off talking about it until a week had passed and by then I realized I didn't want to tell on him. Being a lover of books myself, I knew how he felt. And I know, too, that while the kids in Miss Freeman's classes are getting better about it, most of the other kids in school still enjoy making fun of those of us who like to read. So I didn't say anything. But in class I started to watch Jerry furtively, checking to see if I could see any signs of reading addiction.

Then, on Friday it was my turn to stay after school and clean the blackboard and erasers in the English room. I took the erasers outside to clap them together to get out the chalk dust. When I brought them back in and put them in the cupboard, I took the blackboard rag into the lavatory and got it wet in the sink, then came back and started wiping down the board. The teacher was busy correcting papers at her desk.

"Miss Freeman," I asked, "do you know how much Jerry reads besides the assignments you give us?"

Surprised, she looked up from her work. "Why do you ask?"

"I don't know," I mumbled, "I just wondered. He told me

he likes to read, but I didn't believe him. Now, I've been kinda watching him in class and I'm not sure any more. He never raises his hand when you call for volunteers, but if you just call on him, he always knows the answer. And sometimes I've seen him slip a book under his jacket when the bell rings for the next class."

"You're quite observant, Emma. I was under the impression you don't like Jerry. Why have you been watching him so closely?"

"I'm not sure. We all thought he was dumb and we call him 'stupid,' but I don't think that's right anymore. He dropped *Call of The Wild* a couple of weeks ago when he was at our place and when I practically accused him of stealing it, he told me it's his and he was reading it for the third time. I didn't believe him then, but I think I was wrong. I think maybe he's like me and does like to read."

"Does it make a difference whether or not he likes to read?"

"Well," I hesitated, "I know it shouldn't. And I know we've been mean to him. But, somehow, it makes him seem—oh, I don't know—maybe not so dumb after all. It seems like he must be pretty smart, and maybe some of the rest of us are the dumb ones. I'm not sure that makes any sense. Do you understand what I'm trying to say?"

"Yes, I think I do." Miss Freeman waited so long I thought she wasn't going to talk any more. Then she continued, "I think it's safe to tell you and not have you repeat it to the others. Jerry does like to read. He only has that one book of his own, so I try to find others for him to read, too. When he's finished with each book he slips it back to me and we talk about it after school. Then he waits until I get another one for him. He knows what all of you think of him and he knows that if the others find out he likes to read, they'll probably tease him even more. So he tries to hide the books before anyone sees him. How much do you know about Jerry, Emma?"

"Only what Ivy told me. She said her mama found out that his parents don't want him anymore so his aunt and uncle said he could live here with them. Is that true? It seems kinda funny that parents wouldn't want their own children."

"Well, that's partly true, although there's more to it than that. He's actually a very bright boy, much brighter than any of you give him credit for. But he doesn't want to call any more attention to himself, so he doesn't let the other students know how intelligent he is."

Looking at the clock she said, "It's getting late and you need to get home. Maybe I've said more than I should but I'm trusting you not to discuss this conversation with others. I've come to know you better these past two months, too, and I'm aware that you, also, hide your real feelings and your acuity when you're around your classmates. I grew up in a small town and I know what it's like to be different, so I believe I understand your feelings. In fact, you remind me a little of myself when I was your age." She turned back to her papers, "Hurry and get your coat. Your mother will be wondering where you are."

I remind her of herself? I walked toward home stunned. How could she possibly think that? She's pretty and thin and everybody likes her. That's not a bit like me. She might know I hide my real thoughts from other kids, but I'm certainly not like her in any other way.

Still, I was so flattered by her words that my feet barely touched the ground all the way home.

Chapter Three

"Did you hear about what Sally Oliver did last night?" Ivy's eyes sparkled with malice as we walked to school.

"No. What did she do?" From the glee in Ivy's voice it must have been shocking.

"Well, everybody thinks she's simple-minded but mama says she's crazy like a fox. She says Sally just wants people to think she's slow-witted so she can get away with things decent people wouldn't dream of doing. She says even if Sally does act childish, she's still twenty-five years old and should know better."

I wondered if Ivy was ever going to get to the point. I knew she was dragging her juicy gossip out so I would ask her to tell what Sally had done. But I wasn't going to give her the satisfaction this time. I just kept quiet and waited.

Finally she couldn't hold it any longer. "She got ready for bed with her blinds up! That's what she did!"

"What's such a big deal about that? Lots of people don't pull their blinds down at night." I could be petty, too, I decided. Although by now, I was just as curious as Ivy wanted me to be.

"Sometimes you are so dumb, Em! Of course they leave their blinds up. But not in their bedrooms when they're getting undressed! And that's what Sally did! She took off ALL her clothes and put on her nightgown with her bedroom blinds up and her light on!"

"How do you know that? Did you see her?"

"Course not, silly. But mama said she talked to a neighbor who talked to a cousin who said one of the men he works with saw Sally getting undressed."

"Her bedroom is clear upstairs, for criminy sakes. He must have had to look hard to see her. Why didn't he just walk on past?" Although I knew that nobody would walk past an exhibition like that.

But Ivy saw through me. "Are you kidding?! Even YOU would have stopped to watch if you'd seen her."

I hoped I wouldn't have, but I wasn't sure. After all, I know looking at a naked body is a sin, but I'm not sure I'd be strong enough to resist a peek.

I thought about Sally as we continued on to school while Ivy chattered away. Mr. Oliver died years ago. Ivy had told me her mother said Mrs. Oliver drove her husband to his grave. But when I asked mama about it, she just gave an exasperated sigh and told me not to believe everything certain busybodies in town had to say.

Anyway, Mrs. Oliver had raised Freddie and Sally alone and supported them by turning her home into a boardinghouse. Mrs. Oliver is a thin-lipped, sarcastic woman who complained whenever children got near her flowers or dogs ran through her yard, so us kids had learned to stay away from her. But my mother had always been nice to her and said sometimes people don't know how hard life can be for some people. As I got older I wondered if she meant Sally being kinda crazy and Freddie being drunk all the time. But I didn't ask mama about them. She'd have told me to practice minding my own business. And I didn't want to hear that.

The whole school was buzzing all day with the gossip about Sally Oliver. I figure Ivy's older sister has been as busy telling kids as Ivy has been.

At noon as we sat trading goodies from our lunch sacks with each other, the talk just danced along. Once, I happened to glance at Jerry sitting over in a corner alone. I thought I saw a disgusted expression on his face. But when he noticed me looking at him, he quickly made his face go blank.

Later in the afternoon I was nearly late getting to geography. As I hurried down the hall, Jerry spoke from behind me, "Are you enjoying Ivy's story about Sally?"

I turned in surprise. "No... Yes... I don't know. It's none of your business anyway!"

But it was hard to concentrate in class. I kept thinking about his look of disgust and his question to me. Do I enjoy poor Sally being the butt of all those jokes? I began to realize that, although I've been just as curious as everybody else, I've been more uncomfortable than usual. I wonder if we're not all miserable and mean-minded when we glory in someone else's wretchedness. I didn't sleep well that night.

Next day was the day before Thanksgiving and we were through with school at noon. I was still thinking about the pleasure we'd enjoyed at Sally's expense and I didn't want to walk home with Ivy. So I hung around after class dawdling as I put my work away and got my books ready to take home. I was distracted and not paying attention to my surroundings, when I heard a frightened gasp.

I looked up and saw Miss Freeman back away from the window and scurry toward her desk like she was trying to find a place to hide. With panic in her eyes, she looked blindly about the room.

"Miss Freeman, are you all right?"

She seemed not to see me for a minute. Then she whispered, "Emma, if that man coming up the street comes in asking for someone, please don't mention my name to him."

Without waiting for a reply, she grabbed her coat and was gone.

I walked over to the window and saw a tall, blond, really good-looking man searching each of the school windows that faced the street. Instinctively I shuddered and pulled back. I realized it was probably Miss Freeman's reaction to the man that spooked me, but that didn't take away my fear.

I quickly pulled on my coat and gathered up my books, but just as I got to the bottom of the stairs, there stood the man blocking my way.

"What's the matter, young lady? You look like you've seen a ghost."

Embarrassed, I took a deep breath and looked up into the deepest blue eyes I've ever seen. They seemed to glow with blue fire. I stood spell-bound, unable to move. A strange power emanated from this ruggedly handsome man which seemed to hold me fast.

I finally found my tongue. "No sir. I'm just late and need to get home." The evenness of my voice surprised me. But I was afraid if I said another word the quivering I was feeling would break through.

He looked unwaveringly at me. "Sure, little lady. But first tell me where I can find Mrs. Bond's room."

"Who?!" I was truly confused. "There's no Mrs. Bond teaching here."

"Are you sure? She's a plump little thing with red hair and green eyes."

Even though only the green eyes fit Miss Freeman's description, somehow I was sure he meant her.

"No, there's no one like that named Mrs. Bond here." I hoped I wouldn't be struck dead for the half-truth. But I knew, without knowing how, Miss Freeman was in serious danger.

He stared at me a minute longer and then stepped aside. I walked through the front door, forcing myself not to break into a run for home, glad tomorrow is Thanksgiving. I'm not ready to face Miss Freeman again with all these strange questions racing around in my head.

As I passed Oliver's I wondered if Miss Freeman was there in her room. And I wondered what she would do if that man came there looking for her. Preoccupied, I didn't see Jerry standing by the tree across from the post office.

"Wait up a minute, Emma. I want to talk to you."

I didn't want to talk to him, but felt impelled to stop. I couldn't figure out what was happening to me or what I was doing.

Jerry looked at me. "Are you all right? You look like you've seen a ghost."

That's the second time I've been told that. I snapped back without thinking, "You'd look like you'd seen a ghost, too, if you'd seen what just happened!"

I snapped my mouth shut. What a dumb thing to say! And to Jerry, yet. "Just leave me alone. I need to go home."

He looked hurt. "I'm sorry, Emma. I've been waiting for you here so I could apologize for what I said about Ivy's gossip. I know you're not mean like she is, and I'm sorry for what I said."

I was dumbfounded. This was the strangest thing I had ever heard Jerry say.

"Well, you are right. We are mean to talk about poor Sally. I'm sorry I was rude just now. Something scary just happened and I'm kinda shook up."

I couldn't believe I was saying all this to him. It's almost like we're friends. I stood there puzzled, not understanding myself at all anymore.

Jerry seemed to read my thoughts. "Did you run into that stranger who has been looking for a Mrs. Bond?"

"Yes. How did you know?"

"He's been asking around about her. Too bad he missed Greeley's." He laughed sourly. "Now THERE he would have been bound to find out something."

A shiver ran through me. "Did he describe this Mrs. Bond to anybody?"

"Not that I heard. He's just been asking if she lives here."

Jerry watched my face carefully as he said quietly, "You know something, don't you. I watched that man and there's something fishy about him. But you already know that, don't you?"

"Yes. But don't ask me any more. I can't talk about it right now." I couldn't resist a quick glance over my shoulder. But the street was empty.

"That's okay. I won't ask anything. But remember, you can trust me." He hesitated. "And I want to help Miss Freeman as much as you do."

With that he turned and walked away, leaving me wondering just how much he has figured out.

The next afternoon we enjoyed a good Thanksgiving dinner. My grandma had come to stay for a week. We all love having her around. I especially like it when she tells stories about her pioneer childhood.

As Mama cleared the table, grandma and I began on the

dishes. Daddy and the boys had gone out to milk the cows and there was a peaceful, safe feeling there in our warm little house.

"Livvy, did Rebecca get away all right?"

Mama looked sharply at grandma. "Yes." Her expression said 'not in front of Emma.'

What not in front of me, I thought. "Who is grandma talking about and why can't you talk in front of me?" Mama could hear the annoyance in my voice.

Grandma spoke up quickly, "It's nothing, Emma. I was just asking about a friend of your mother's."

"Mama doesn't have any friends named Rebecca..." I stopped short, remembering seeing that name in one of Miss Freeman's books.

My voice shook as I tried to contain my tears. "Why do you all treat me like a baby? Something's going on around here and you all act like I'm not old enough to understand it. It has something to do with Miss Freeman, doesn't it? And that man who was here yesterday looking for her?"

Mama said quietly, "Sit down, Emma. You're right. I haven't told you what's happening. Even now I'm not sure how much I should say."

"Well, if you're afraid I'll tell, you can stop worrying. I'm not a tattletale."

"I know you're not, sweetheart. But there are people in this town who delight in destroying a person's good name if they can. And there are others who desperately need to keep their private lives private." She paused. "What do you know about a man looking for Miss Freeman? Why didn't you tell me about that?"

"I wasn't sure of it myself." And then I explained what happened after school yesterday and what Jerry had said to me on the way home.

"There's something really scary about that man and I don't know why. He's awfully good-looking and he talked nice to me. But there's something about him that frightens me. I didn't say anything about it because I wasn't sure it wasn't just my imagination." I looked into mama's sympathetic eyes, "But I didn't imagine Miss Freeman's fear."

Grandma stood there looking pensive. "Little Emma, there are some things in this life that are too hard and too sad to think about. Why don't you go out and see how the milking is coming along and I'll finish these dishes."

"No mother," said mama gently. "I think Emma deserves an explanation and I believe she can keep what we say in confidence." She looked steadily at me. "You must promise never to say a word."

I nodded in agreement, wondering if I really wanted to hear something as serious as this.

"Miss Freeman isn't her real name. She was once married to that man you saw yesterday. He was very cruel to her and she finally left him. He had told her that if she ever dared to leave he would find her and kill her. That's why she lives under an assumed name and why she was so terrified when she spotted him yesterday."

"But how can that be, mama? Why doesn't she just go to the sheriff?"

"That man is a sheriff. And she's afraid no one will dare to stand up to him. No one ever came to her defense when she was married to him, even though she tried to get help then. That's why she's afraid. She hasn't got anywhere to turn."

"But what about her own parents? Why doesn't she go back and live with them?"

"They died a few years ago, never really believing her husband was so dangerous. They just thought she wasn't treating him right and he was punishing her as a husband should."

I had to think about that. I know that a wife is supposed to obey her husband and make his life happy. But this didn't sound right.

"Mama, that's wrong, isn't it? Even if a wife is supposed to obey her husband, isn't he also supposed to treat her nice? Like you and daddy, I mean?"

"Yes, Emma, that's the way it should be. But it doesn't always work that way. And this is one of those cases that people don't like to think about, so no one talks about it."

"Well, how do you know all this? I know you and Miss

Freeman, or whatever her name is, know each other, but I didn't know you were that friendly with her."

"That's the way we wanted it. We're not trying to hide anything from you, but I felt it would be better not to involve you in our friendship. Your friend, Ivy, tells things she hears at home and I didn't want you to have to worry about trying to keep secrets from her."

"But I do keep secrets from her! I know she's a gossip just like her mother and I never trust her with things that are really important to me."

"I'm glad you're so wise. I guess I just didn't realize you've grown up so much. I'm sorry you were hurt by this. Try to forget it."

"I'll try, but I don't think I will forget it. Besides, how will Miss Freeman keep that man from finding her? Where is she now?"

"Daddy drove her to a safe place not far from town yesterday when she rushed here straight from school. When he got back he checked and found out that a man was asking about a Mrs. Bond. Daddy intercepted him and convinced him that the woman he's looking for isn't in this town. Mr. Bond finally left in his truck. I guess he'll keep looking for her, but we think she'll be safe here now."

I hope so. Oh, how I hope so!

Chapter Four

"What are you getting for Christmas?"

I turned quickly, glancing around the gym.

"Don't worry, they've all gone."

Shamefacedly I turned to face him. I would never figure out how Jerry was able to read my thoughts. He knows I'm still getting used to having him for a friend. And he knows, too, that confidence doesn't come easily for me.

These past two weeks we've talked together more than I ever dreamed possible. But I still made sure no one saw us. And I made sure Ivy didn't know about our blossoming friendship. I'm not brave enough to face her ridicule. He understands this and always makes sure no one is around when we talk.

The seventh and eighth grades had just finished practicing for our Christmas program in the gym. But now all the other kids were on their way home. Jerry and I stood there watching as the windows began to darken in the early winter gloom.

"I'm hoping for some riding boots, but I'm afraid we won't be able to afford them. What about you? What do you want?"

Jerry paused. "I'd really like a pair of ice-skates. I

wouldn't even care if they were the clamp on kind. But I haven't said anything. Uncle Jim and Aunt Emily have done so much for me already that I really can't ask them for anything more."

"Why are you living with them? You never talk about your own family or your life before coming here."

Jerry waited so long I thought he wasn't going to answer. Then he spoke so quietly I could barely hear him.

"I'd like to forget about my life before I came here. You wouldn't understand, anyway." He hesitated. "You've got a real neat family, you know that?"

"Yeah, I guess so." Although frankly I thought my brothers were a pain in the neck sometimes. "But you're not answering my question. Why do you live here? And why do you want to forget about your family?"

"Emma, you and I are friends now and I'm glad. But there are some things even friends shouldn't ask. So do you mind if we just forget about it."

I retorted angrily, "Well, if that's the way you want it, Jerry Harris, that's the way you'll get it! But don't bother me any more! I know friends don't tell each other everything. But I thought you'd at least tell me about your family. After all, I'm not Ivy Greeley, you know. I'm just me—plain old Emma Williams—a dopey kid who thought since you know my family so well, I ought to know a little bit about yours. Just forget I asked!"

I ran out the door and down the stairs, mad at myself for caring whether Jerry told me about himself or not. Stupid jerk, I thought. Who needs him anyway?'

I half expected him to come after me and apologize and explain. But he didn't.

When I got home I was still in a rotten mood.

"What's the matter, twerp?" Bruce asked. "You act like you could chew nails."

"None of your darn business!" I yelled.

Mama looked up from the stove where she was cutting potatoes into a kettle. "Just a minute, young lady. If you have a problem, don't come home and take it out on your family. What's gotten into you?"

"Nothing," I grumbled. "I'm just tired. That darned program is too long and I've got too much homework to do and I'm tired of being the only one around here who has to be in early every night."

I couldn't believe it! Tears filled my eyes and came streaming down my face. I couldn't decide if I was more mad or more humiliated.

"Come on, Emma," mama said calmly, "let's go into the bedroom. I think we need to talk."

She shut the door and we sat down on the bed. With mama's arm around my shoulders, I suddenly felt so ashamed of myself. Here I was wanting to be treated like a grown-up, and still acting like a baby.

Mama didn't say anything. She handed me a handkerchief from her apron pocket and sat there quietly while I finished blubbering. Then, "Those aren't the real reasons you're upset, are they? What's really bothering you, sweetheart?"

So I told her about my growing friendship with Jerry and how I had just thrown it all away.

"You know, when Jerry used to try to talk to me, I was so stupid I didn't want Ivy or the other kids to think he was my friend. So I treated him awful. But he still tried to be nice to me. And now that I've got to know him better, I'm ashamed because I still don't want the other kids to know he's my friend. And what's worse, he knows that and never lets on about us being friends when other kids are around. I'm such a jerk I don't deserve any friends!"

"Well, Emma, it sounds like you really are growing up. And it is hard. Don't ever kid yourself otherwise. There are lots of times when it seems better all around to take the easy road. But a truly mature person comes to understand that the easiest road isn't necessarily the right road."

"Why does it still bother me to let Ivy know I'm friends with Jerry? Why can't I just ignore her and do what I want?"

"Oh, I think it's mostly habit. You two have been friends all your lives. And all that time you've let Ivy take the lead, following behind and not letting her know how you really feel about a lot of things. And I don't blame you. It's very hard to be different and to feel like you'll be all alone if you don't hold onto the only best friend you've ever had.

"But, you see, there comes a time when you have to take hold of things and make some tough decisions. Nobody can do that for you. We can help you and be here for you. But you're the one who has to finally decide whether or not you're strong enough to stand on your own two feet."

"What if I'm not strong enough, mama? What if I'll never be strong enough to stop tagging along behind Ivy?"

"My dear, sweet daughter. You don't know it, but you're already much stronger than you realize. You've learned not to share your deepest thoughts with Ivy. And you acquired some hard information at Thanksgiving time that you handled very well. You'll see. There'll come a time when you can let go of the dependence you have on Ivy. You'll still be friends, but it will be as equals, not as leader and subordinate."

We sat there awhile, both immersed in our own thoughts. It was comforting to know that mama had confidence in me. I hoped, someday, I'd have confidence in myself.

"Mama, why wouldn't Jerry tell me about his family? Do you know about them?"

"Yes, I know some things—certainly not all—but some of his past. But, Emma, I don't think I'm the one to tell you about that. Jerry is right about friends not having to tell everything. And when he feels secure in your friendship, he'll tell you what he wants to tell. You just have to be patient and not try to pry.

"I can tell you this. His childhood is very painful for him to think about. When he's ready, he'll talk about it. And if he's never ready, that should be all right, too. Sometimes we put things that distress us way down in the deepest recesses of our minds where we don't have to look at them. Jerry has to make the decision about how much he wants to share."

She stood up. "Come on, let's go set the table. That soup must be ready by now and daddy and the boys will be coming in hungry any minute."

Three days before Christmas we gave our program. Practically everybody in town came. The gym was filled. Adults sat on the folding benches the boys had set up, and children sat on the floor in front of the stage.

Jerry had stayed away from me since our quarrel and I hadn't done anything to make amends.

"What are you going to do after the program?" Ivy asked as we waited for the curtain to part.

"Go home," I said. "The program won't be over until nearly nine and you know as well as I do that I can't stay out later than that."

"Honestly, Emma, I can't believe your mother is so fussy. Doesn't she realize you'll be a teenager next summer? Your birthday is two weeks before mine and I've been able to stay out late for a long time."

Suddenly I was fed up. "Well, Ivy, I frankly don't care

whether you stay out late or not. I think your mother could learn a few things from mine about raising kids!"

She looked at me with her mouth open. I had never challenged her or criticized her mother before. But I realized I was sick and tired of her condescending attitude toward me. It dawned on me that I really didn't give a darn whether we stayed friends anymore.

She must have sensed something in my manner because she stopped short, looked at me for a minute, then said, "Well, you don't have to be so huffy. I didn't mean to insult your mother. I never thought you'd get so upset about such a little thing."

My mind whirled. What? Is this really Ivy talking? She's backing down to me. She's never done that before. Maybe she's not as sure of herself as I've always thought. Maybe mama is right. Maybe I can stand up to Ivy and still stay friends. My sense of deliverance was overwhelming.

"Forget it," I said quietly. "It doesn't matter."

But it did matter! I was giddy with delight as my insecurities began to crumble around me. I had never in my life felt so good.

As we all started down the stairs after the program, I saw Jerry walking with his aunt and uncle a couple of steps ahead of us. His little cousins were holding onto his hands.

"Mama, can I come home in a little while? I want to see if Jerry will talk to me."

She looked at me with a warm glow in her eyes. "Yes, Emma. I think it'll be okay for you to stay out a few more minutes. Just don't be too late."

"Jerry," I called. "Wait up. I want to talk to you." He stopped in mid-step, glancing at all the people around us like he couldn't believe what he was hearing.

"Will you see if you can be a little late. I'd like to talk, please."

He still looked stunned, but said something quietly to his aunt. She nodded and took the children's hands while he stepped to the side of the stairs to wait for me.

As I grabbed his hand and pulled him outside, I saw Ivy staring at us. I grinned and waved at her. "Goodnight, Ivy. See you tomorrow."

When we got outside we ran around the side of the building and sat down on the low wall around the playground.

"Emma, do you feel all right?" Jerry still looked puzzled.

"Yes!" I laughed. "I've never felt better!"

We had to go to school until noon the next day and, to tell the truth, I don't think I learned a thing in any of my classes. I had never felt so good. Jerry and I were friends again. And Ivy was no better than me. And I didn't owe anybody an explanation about what I like to do or who I choose to be friends with. It was like I had been carrying something really heavy around for the past few weeks, and now I felt free and light and secure. Is this what it's like to really have the Christmas spirit, I asked myself? If so, I want to hold on to it forever.

Chapter Five

Winter seemed to go on forever. Snow started falling Christmas Eve and didn't stop for three days. Everything was covered with a deep blanket of white. When the storm dissipated, the cold moved in making the earth look like it was covered with diamonds. We kids loved every minute of it.

We took sleds part way up the mountain and made a spectacular sleigh-riding path. We cleaned the snow off the frozen creek and ice skated to our hearts content. Some of us were lucky enough to have the new shoe skates, but most of the kids still had to strap their skates onto the soles of their shoes.

I got new riding boots for Christmas after all. And not only that, there under the tree was a beautiful pair of tan riding pants. 'Jodhpurs' the tag said. A wonderfully sophisticated name for a simple pair of pants. I loved it!

Jerry was so surprised when he got new shoe ice-skates for Christmas. He couldn't figure out how his aunt and uncle knew he wanted them. I didn't let on I had whispered his wish to his aunt when she asked me in the store before Christmas.

"Did Santa Claus come to your house Christmas Eve?" I asked as we skated together.

"Yes. My little cousins were wide-eyed with excitement." Jerry smiled. "Does he leave little sacks of candy and nuts at every house in town, or just those with little kids?"

"He goes to every house. Sometimes it's the same Santa for a few years in a row." When I started to laugh he looked at me, perplexed.

"I'm just remembering the year Freddie Oliver was Santa. I must have been about five years old. After he left our house I asked mama why Santa had such a hard time walking straight and why he had to hold onto the railing so tight when he went down our porch steps. My brothers hooted with laughter and even mama and daddy had a hard time keeping straight faces. It was a few more years before I understood that Santa, that night, had enjoyed Christmas cheer at some of the other houses before he ever got to ours."

The New Year's Eve Dance was lots of fun. This time I enjoyed dancing with Jerry as much as Ivy had pretended to at the Deer Hunt Dance. And he really isn't such a bad dancer. Either he has practiced lately or my opinion was wrong before. Maybe a little of both.

"Happy 1939," I called to Jerry when school resumed again. And I meant it, too.

"The same to you," he grinned back as we passed each other in the hall.

School continued much the same as before the holidays

except now Jerry didn't sit alone at lunchtime. And when Ivy had her Valentine's party, Jerry was invited along with the rest of us. He seemed to blend into our school group effortlessly. As though he had been going to school with us forever.

But he still held part of himself aloof. Whenever any of us got talking about something our family was doing, Jerry was part of the group, but somehow separate. None of the other kids noticed his subtle withdrawal. Or, if they did, nobody said anything. But I noticed it and tried to remember what mama had said about respecting his privacy. I didn't ask him any more questions about his life before coming to Grassville. And he never volunteered any information.

Winter finally turned to spring. Sleigh riding and ice skating gave way to roller skating and kick-the-can. We put our coats and galoshes and long underwear away for another year, got to wear anklets again and were glad to have more time for play as the days grew longer.

"Mama, who are those strange people I saw go into the store today?"

"They're Gypsies. You've seen them before."

"When?" I couldn't remember ever seeing those dusky-skinned people whose women wore gathered, bright-colored skirts and had large gold earrings dangling from their ears.

"Maybe you were too young to remember. They come to town every few years. Don't go around them."

I looked at her with irritation. "I wasn't planning to. They don't look too friendly to me. Where do they stay, anyway?"

"Usually down in the cottonwood grove south of town. There's a fresh water spring there."

"What are they doing here?"

"They travel all over the country. I guess all over the world. The men sometimes work at odd jobs, but mostly they gamble to get a little money, or the women tell fortunes for those who believe in that sort of thing. Then they move on. They never stay any place very long."

But Ivy had lots more to tell about the Gypsies next day at school. "They put curses on people and steal anything they can get their hands on. Mama says they even steal children."

"Why would they do that?" I had seen some of their ragged little waifs tagging along behind some of them. "What would they want more kids for?"

"They teach them to be pickpockets and then send them out to big cities all over the country. Mama says we have to keep a close watch on all the children while they're around."

I wondered if Ivy knew what she was talking about. It seemed kinda funny to me. But other things she had said over the years had proved to be closer to the truth than I thought, so maybe she was right this time, too.

Miss Freeman and I had never discussed my encounter with her ex-husband. But I knew she was aware of it. Mama briefly informed me that she and Miss Freeman had talked about the events of last November. Miss Freeman's smile seemed more poignant whenever we talked, but her manner was still reserved and we were still student and teacher.

I never mentioned what I had learned to Ivy or Jerry, either. He would have understood and kept his mouth shut, but I was determined to keep my promise to mama.

"Mikey's missing!"
"Who?"
"You know! The little Peters boy!"

The town was in an uproar. Three year old Mikey hadn't been seen since soon after lunch and his mother was frantic.

People helped check every house to see if he was there. But no one had seen him.

"The toilets! Look and see if he's fallen down a toilet!" These were a major worry for parents with little children. Only a few houses in town had indoor bathrooms. Most of us still walked to the outhouse, regardless of the season.

But this search, too, was fruitless.

Then someone mentioned the Gypsies.

In no time at all a large crowd of men gathered in front of the store. Some carried pitchforks. Others had shovels or axes.

"Good heavens!" mama exclaimed. "What do they think they're doing?! Someone could get hurt or killed!"

But a madness seemed to fill the air. It wasn't just a crowd of familiar townspeople anymore. It was an angry, seething mob.

Mama had warned me to stay away from the Gypsies but, knowing that's where the mob was heading, I slipped out the back door and joined a bunch of kids following the enraged crowd. We stayed out of sight but watched as the mob marched straight to the Gypsy camp.

It was obvious the Gypsies had been warned and were waiting. The women and children were out of sight, but the men were grouped together on the road in front of the trees.

"What do you want here?" A huge man, who seemed to be their leader, stood in front of the others. "Why do you come and bother us?"

"We want the kid!" someone yelled.

"What kid? What are you talking about?"

Someone else shouted, "You know what we're talking about! You stole one of our kids and we want him back!"

Watching from behind a clump of trees, I was terrified. Fury crackled around both groups like lightening dancing between them.

"We don't have your child." Another Gypsy stepped forward. His voice wasn't loud yet it carried unspoken danger. "We don't steal children, regardless of what you think." The menace in his voice seemed to freeze everyone.

Then Mr. Peters started forward, his axe held in front of

him. "We don't believe you! Either you move and let us search your wagons or we'll slaughter every man, woman and child in this camp!"

As the men surged forward, a shot rang out. The Gypsy leader bellowed, "Take one more step and you're dead!" Guns and knives appeared simultaneously in the hands of every Gypsy.

"No!" cried a voice from the direction of town. "Stop! Mikey's okay! Stop!"

Everyone turned as Jerry ran to stand between the two groups of men. His breathing was ragged, each word an effort. "Mikey's home. He climbed up on the mountain behind the school and fell asleep on one of the boulders. He's home now, safe and sound."

"Are you sure? This isn't a trick, is it?"

"No," his breathing was less labored now, "it's not a trick. Yes, I'm sure. Everybody can go home now. Mikey's okay."

I caught up with Jerry as he wearily started back toward town. When we were away from the others I asked, "Who found Mikey? And why did you put yourself right in the middle of those men? You could have been hurt."

"I found him," he replied quietly. "I've seen him play on the mountain there before. So I went looking for him." He continued grimly, "I know I could have been hurt, but somebody had to stop that stupidity. I know what happens when people get violent. It was all such a dumb mistake."

I looked at him as we continued on home. We didn't talk any more. But I knew he had opened a little part of his own life to me.

Next morning the Gypsies were gone.

Chapter Six

"Emma, will you please go out and see if you can find two more eggs. I want to put a cake in the oven when this bread is done."

I was glad to escape from the hot kitchen into the cool April air. The coal stove was fine for keeping the kitchen warm during the winter but once summer drew near, we all dreaded its heat. And yet, without a fire in the stove, there would be no hot water in the water heater or cooked meals. So we live with it. We always have. After all, there are only two houses in town that have the new electric cook stoves—Dr. Louganis's and Greeley's.

Nobody was surprised when Greeleys got their stove last year. Mrs. Greeley was always the first to have any new appliance or furniture.

And Ivy and her sister were just like their mama. Always the first with new shoes and new clothes and new things. I remember when Ivy and I were eight years old and the most beautiful doll I'd ever seen appeared in the big front window of the store two weeks before Christmas. How I coveted that doll! But even then, I wasn't surprised when Ivy showed it to me Christmas day.

I hooked the gate in the fence around the chicken coop

securely and went gingerly into the coop. I looked in all the empty nests but there were no eggs. I hated to slide my hand under any of the three hens settled on their nests, but there was nothing else to do. Mama wanted the eggs and I knew not to go back into the house without checking.

Nothing under the first hen. She grumbled as I disturbed her. I didn't care about that, I just didn't want to get pecked.

Nothing under the second hen, either. Rats. Should I forget the last one? She was always irritable and as likely as not to peck me if I came near.

I turned to go. I could tell mama that I looked under both hens and that would be the truth. But I knew, and I knew she would know, it isn't the whole truth. My mama is better at seeing through fibs than anybody I've ever seen. Nope. I'll have to search that third nest.

Walking carefully and keeping my eyes focused tight on the fidgety hen, I began to talk quietly, "It's okay. I'm not going to hurt you. I wouldn't disturb you if I had any other choice. Now missy, don't look at me like that. Just let me check your nest and I'll be on my way."

All the time the hen watched me with her beady eyes. I swear she knows I'm afraid of her. I slid my hand slowly toward her nest, careful not to make any quick movements. I inched my fingers gently through the straw and felt her warm feathers.

Suddenly she flew up squawking and fluttering her wings and I knew for sure I was in deep trouble. Before I could bolt and run I forced myself to glance quickly into the nest. Bingo! Two eggs lay there just as nice as could be.

I scooped them up, jumped through the coop door, and made a mad dash for the gate. Now all the chickens were clucking and cackling and hopping all over the place. I slipped through the gate without letting any of them out and stood for a minute to catch my breath.

"What in the world was all that ruckus? You didn't let any of the chickens loose, did you?"

"No, mama. They were just complaining about my visit is all." And I handed her the eggs, glad that gathering them every day was Bruce's job and not mine.

Next week would be Easter. I could hardly wait. I loved the new dress mama made me from the material grandma sent. It was pink organdy with a ruffle around the bottom of the skirt and lace around the sleeves and collar. It was the most beautiful dress I had ever seen.

As I looked in the mirror and preened, I realized Aunt Betsy was right. My baby fat had disappeared during the winter.

I felt a little guilty knowing that mama is the one who should have a new dress, not me. But I just couldn't stop the pride bursting inside me. I had already seen Ivy's new Easter dress and it isn't near as pretty as mine.

School seemed to drag. I thought the week would never end. Then on Thursday morning, Ivy didn't show up at our usual meeting place so I walked over to her house and knocked on the door.

Mr. Greeley opened the door a crack and quietly said, "Ivy won't be going to school today, Emma." I thought I heard sobbing coming from somewhere in the house but he shut the door so fast I couldn't be sure.

That's funny. How can anybody in that house ever cry about anything? Mr. Greeley has been the store and confectionery owner as long as I can remember. The Greeleys always have everything they ever want. And whatever they want is always the biggest and best and newest in town.

Both Ivy and her sister Daisy, who is two years older, have always been very pretty, and popular besides. Crying in that house? No. I must have imagined it. And yet, something's the matter.

Next morning Ivy met me same as usual but didn't say two words all the way to school. I had never seen her so quiet and so long faced.

"What's the matter? Cat got your tongue?"

"Just shut up and leave me alone, Emma."

"For crying out loud. What's got into you? I didn't mean anything. I've just never seen you act this way."

She kept her eyes on the ground. "I just don't feel very good."

After school was out I didn't see Ivy anywhere, so I started on home alone. When I got over to Main Street there she stood, waiting for me on the corner. "I'm sorry for snapping at you, Emma."

Was this Ivy talking? I stood there bewildered. "That's okay. I'm sorry you don't feel good. Are you coming down with something?"

"I wish it was as simple as that."

She started walking. I thought she wasn't going to say anything more. Then she stopped. "It's Daisy. She's going to Denver to visit my aunt."

That didn't seem like something to feel bad about to me. I'd love to spend a summer some place like that. "Lucky her! Will she stay all summer?"

"You don't understand. She's leaving on the train tomorrow."

"Tomorrow? What about school?"

"She'll finish this year over there."

I still thought it sounded fun. Imagine going to a big city and getting to meet a whole bunch of new kids!

Then it hit me. Ivy was jealous. "It won't be too bad. Maybe you can go next time. And you've still got your friends here. Besides, it'll only be a little over a month."

In a flat, toneless voice Ivy whispered, "No. She's going to stay there till after Halloween."

"Halloween! Why so long?" Maybe it wouldn't be so fun after all. That's a long time to be away from home.

"My aunt has this big house and with my uncle gone on

business so much, she needs someone to be there with her." Her words came out like she'd memorized them for a part in a play. It was making less sense all the time.

"Well, maybe your family can take a trip to see her this summer. It isn't like she'll be gone forever."

Ivy sighed. "No, it won't be forever." Then she added fiercely, "It shouldn't have to be at all. Stupid, dumb Daisy!"

I thought about Ivy's outburst as I walked on home. It seemed so out of character for her to be that upset about Daisy's vacation. Just goes to show you don't always know people...even your best friend.

"By the way, Tom, I invited the Ruiz family to ride with us to the Easter picnic tomorrow."

"That's fine. What time did you tell them we'd pick them up?"

"As close to noon as we can make it. Their church is over by ten but I told them we won't be out until nearly noon."

So mama invited Mary's family. Well, it doesn't surprise me. Mama had become friends with Mrs. Ruiz after her illness last fall.

And surprisingly, I don't really mind. I've talked with Mary a few times at school even though the 'tag town' kids still don't mix much with us town kids. But since I discovered that Ivy's opinion isn't essential to my survival, I don't feel threatened about having the Ruiz family go with us to the Easter picnic.

We didn't have Sunday School. Instead, we had our Easter program. It was really good this year. The Primary children sang three songs, a mixed quartet sang *He Is Rise,* I played a variation of *I Know That My Redeemer Lives* on the organ, and the congregation sang three songs. There were a couple of talks about the real meaning of Easter which hit home to me because of my vanity about my new dress. But, all in all, it was a good meeting.

As we were leaving church I asked Jerry if they were coming to the picnic. "Yeah. It sounds like fun. I've never been on a picnic with a whole town before."

"It's kind of a tradition around here. It must have started years ago cause as far back as I can remember we've done this on Easter."

We got to the picnic grounds up the canyon just as the softball game was starting. I can't bat worth a darn, but I'm good at first base.

While we played ball, the men put together the sawhorses and planks Mr. Kenner, from the sawmill, had brought up in his truck. These were soon converted into long tables. The women covered the boards with tablecloths and then brought out their baskets and boxes and sacks and started filling the table with food.

It was a feast to delight everyone. There was fried chicken and meat loaf and potato salad and spaghetti and cooked green beans and carrots and fresh bread and rolls and pies and cakes and gallons of homemade root beer. We ate until we couldn't stuff in another bite.

I was sorry Ivy was missing all the fun. I hadn't seen any of the Greeleys since Friday. Maybe they were still getting used to Daisy leaving.

"Mama, is it okay if I take a little hike up the mountain? I won't go far."

"Just be sure you stay away from the south face. The rocks there are unstable."

I guess I've heard that same warning every year. "Don't worry. I'll watch where I'm going."

As I turned to start climbing, I saw Mary watching me. On impulse I said to her, "Do you want to come along?"

She looked at her mother who nodded and said, "Just be careful."

Why do parents always say the same thing? It doesn't matter what we want to do, it's always, "Be careful."

We climbed fast, not talking much. It always makes me feel free and happy to be up in the mountains. I'm so glad we live in a town with mountains close by.

"Do you climb often?" Mary asked shyly.

"Yes. I've been climbing these mountains since I was little. What about you?"

"I love the mountains. We haven't always lived near them so now I climb the one behind our house whenever I can. But that's not very often. Mama needs me to help with the little ones. She's not very strong." I remembered mama saying the same thing about Mrs. Ruiz.

Mary went on hesitantly, "When I'm up above the valley I feel so good. I look out and wish I could visit all the places I've heard about beyond the mountains."

"Hey! Me too! I didn't know you felt like that."

"The kids would laugh at me if they knew. You're the only one I've ever told. But I've seen you climb the mountain sometimes and envied you."

I'll be darned. I learn something new every day. Mary isn't so different after all.

We sat on one of the huge boulders and looked out over town. Mary asked, "Do you ever want to visit other places? I mean not just beyond these mountains, but all over the world?"

"I'd really like that. I'm not sure I'll ever get to but mama says for me not to give up my dreams. She says anything is possible if I work for it hard enough." I laughed, "In fact, any time any of us say we can't do something, mama pulls out a line from a long forgotten joke from her own childhood... 'My Willie can do anything.' We all know that means she believes we can do whatever we want if we work hard for it."

Mary smiled. "No wonder my mother likes her so much. They think alike. When daddy talks about traveling all over the country during the worst of the Depression, I close my eyes and try to picture the places he describes. Course he says it was really bad, always being driven out of one town and another, never knowing if he'd earn enough money to buy food for us. But I still think he's lucky to have seen so many places."

"Didn't you and your mother go with him?"

"No. Most of the time we stayed with my grandma and grandpa. Dad hitched rides on boxcars and slept on the ground in places he called hobo camps. He didn't want us living like that. Did your dad ever do that?"

"No. He stayed right here in town with us. There was never much money but he was able to work enough right here to take care of us."

We sat silently for awhile, wrapped in our private daydreams, wanting time to stand still. Everything was so beautiful and peaceful. The sun slowly moved toward the west. It would soon be time to pack up and head back home. I didn't want this day to end. It was so perfect.

"Let's walk around that tree over there. I want to see the south face I've been warned so much about."

Mary looked at me gravely but didn't say a word. We got to our feet and started walking. I was a few feet ahead of her and not watching where I was going when I felt the shale under me start to give way.

In a split second I was sliding down the mountain heading directly for the cliff edge ahead. Frantically I grabbed the air around me trying to make contact with something. As I neared the top of the cliff, I felt my hand touch something bristly. I closed my fingers around some sagebrush and held on for dear life. Rocks and dirt were sliding all around me. I didn't know if the bush would give way under my weight.

"Emma!" I heard Mary's call off to the left. "Are you all right?"

"For now," I called back. "Don't come any closer! There's no solid ground anywhere!"

I had turned to the side as I was sliding and now reached up with my other hand to grab the bush. My arms felt like they were being pulled out of their sockets and I wasn't sure how much longer I could hold on.

"You'd better go for help, Mary!" Although I knew I'd never be able to hang on that long. I tried to dig my toes into the dirt but it kept sliding out from under me. They say your life passes in front of your eyes when you're about to die but that wasn't what was in my thoughts. I kept hearing mama's warning not to go near the south face. And I kept remembering my smart-aleck reaction about parents who tell their kids to be careful.

"Emma! Can you hear me?"

I angled my head and tried to look up the slope. "Jerry? Where are you?"

"Right here above you. Hold on and we'll try to help you."

"Don't come any closer!" I could feel dirt and little rocks cascading around me again.

"Just hang on!"

In a few seconds I felt something brush my cheek.

"Emma! Can you grab that branch?"

"I don't know. I'll try." My hands were almost numb. I reached out cautiously and tried to wrap the fingers of my right hand around the branch. My hand wouldn't work. I couldn't tighten my fingers.

I opened and closed my hand to try and get life back into it. Then I grabbed for the branch again. Yes! This time my fingers held fast. I was glad for the twigs extending out from the branch even though I could feel slivers puncturing my palm. The twigs were keeping my sweaty hand from sliding off the end.

As soon as I knew my right hand was secure, I began flexing my left. The minute I felt blood flowing through my fingers again, I grabbed the branch with that hand, too.

"Okay! I've got it," I called. "Can you pull me up?"

"We'll start now. Just don't let go whatever you do!"

He had to be kidding. If they found me at the bottom of the cliff, they'd find my fingers stuck tight to that branch.

Inch by inch I felt my self being dragged upwards. I kept trying to find purchase with my feet, but the ground was still unstable. After another upward tug or two all movement stopped.

"Emma, hold on a minute. We need to back up a little."

"Okay. Just don't take too long." I couldn't bring myself to tell them I was losing all feeling in my hands. They were doing everything they could. And I only had myself to blame for the predicament I was in.

I edged my foot to the left and dug in my toe again. There was something hard there! Carefully I slid my foot back and forth and the object didn't budge. Could it be solid rock? I was afraid to hope. I pressed on it harder but it stayed put. I wriggled my other foot closer. The surface was firm.

"Hey! I think I've hit solid ground. Hold on while I see if I can shinny up a little." With my hands holding tight to the branch and my feet snaking over the ground, I finally rolled to a spot where the earth didn't move any more.

I lay there overwhelmed while I tried to unclasp my hands. Jerry and Mary crept gingerly over to where I lay. They both looked exhausted and I saw a trace of tears on Mary's face.

"Are you okay? Can you get up?" Jerry stretched out his hand for me to take.

"I think so." Although my knees were shaking so bad I wasn't sure I could stand if I did make it to my feet.

I started to brush the dirt off my clothes, then looked at my scratched hands and stopped to pull out some of the slivers. "I guess thanks doesn't much say what I'm feeling. If it wasn't for you two, I would be at the bottom of the cliff now."

They both just looked at me. Finally Jerry said, "We probably ought to start back down. Can you walk okay now?"

I nodded, not trusting myself to speak. We started to climb down but I still had a favor to ask. Finally I blurted out, "I know it's not fair to ask you, but..."

"You don't have to say it," Mary interrupted. "We won't tell anyone what happened."

"Thanks," I mumbled, realizing once again that mama knew me better than I knew myself.

As we worked our way down the mountain I asked Jerry how he happened to be there.

"I don't know for sure. After we ate I explored the campgrounds. When I got back to where the others were I looked around and couldn't see you two anywhere. I asked Bruce and he said you'd hiked up the mountain. I sat down to wait for you to get back, but I couldn't relax. So I decided to climb up and see if I could find you."

Mary spoke up, "I'd just turned around to run down for help when I saw Jerry coming up. I called to him to hurry."

We walked in silence for a few minutes. Then Mary spoke again. "I never would have thought to find a branch for you to hold onto. And even if I had, I wouldn't have been able to pull you up by myself. I don't know what I'd have done if Jerry hadn't been there."

"It wasn't just me, Mary. It took you to get me there fast

and it took both of us to pull on that branch."

"Well, I just want you both to know I'll never forget what you did for me. And," I added quietly, "next time I hear 'Be careful,' maybe I'll pay more attention."

Chapter Seven

April ended unseasonably warm and calm. "If this weather keeps up we'll have a scorcher of a summer." People just couldn't seem to talk about anything else.

Except the rumors about Daisy Greeley. I didn't know whether to believe them or not and wasn't about to ask mama. But every time I watched a very subdued Ivy, and every time I saw her mother going quietly about her own business, I wondered.

By the middle of the first week in May the talk had changed to building the dam for the swimming pool. So, early Saturday afternoon we all met at the usual place by the creek above town. The older boys rolled nearby boulders over the steep banks of the creek just below its widest and deepest spot. While they worked, the rest of us gathered up the gunnysacks we'd all saved over the winter and took turns shoveling dirt into them. The ends were tied with pieces of rope and twine and we all tugged, pulled and carried the full gunnysacks to the water's edge. By then the boulders had been fitted as snugly as possible into place across the width of the creek.

The stream was already starting to back up behind the rocks. So now the biggest boys made a line across the creek just in front of the stone dam and the rest of us manhandled the bags of dirt to the person nearest the edge. One by one the filled gunnysacks were lifted and shoved to the next person along the line until all the bags were fitted in and around and on top of the boulders. The gunnysacks were then adjusted and arranged to make the dam as water-tight as possible. It was evening before all the bags were secure but none of us stopped until the job was done.

Now all we had to do was wait for nature to take its course. Our dam measured about six feet high and we knew that by the end of the next week or two, water would be nearly to the top and swimming could begin in earnest.

A small stream of water still trickled through the cracks to continue its journey down through town and beyond. And once the water rose to the top of the dam, it would then overflow and continue down the creek. But soon enough water would be trapped behind the dam to create the only kind of swimming pool most of us had ever known. The water would never be clear enough to see the bottom and the creek sides were steep and slippery, but that pool was where we would jump, dive and swim all summer long. Or, at least until the summer thunderstorms brought floods raging down the creek to destroy our handiwork and cut the creek banks deeper still.

The following Friday we made hurried plans in school to celebrate the building of our swimming pool.

"Are you coming to the wiener roast tonight?" I hoped Ivy would get back to her old self soon. She had been avoiding all after school activities and hadn't showed up when we built the swimming pool last Saturday.

"No, I don't think so. I've got some lessons to catch up on."

But she wouldn't make eye contact as she answered. Too, this was the first time I had ever heard her use schoolwork as an excuse to get out of anything.

"Come on, Ivy. It'll be fun. We're all meeting at the schoolhouse and going up the canyon together."

But she wouldn't budge. "No. I'm not going and I don't want you to keep coaxing. I don't want to go."

I waited, hoping she would say something more or explain why she was being so unyielding. Finally she looked directly at me. "You've heard the rumors about Daisy, haven't you?"

I didn't want to make her feel bad, but I'm not a very good liar. My expression was answer enough.

"Well, they're not true! My aunt really does need Daisy there." She added firmly, "People in this town are mealy-mouthed gossips!"

Hearing that from a Greeley made it real hard for me to keep a straight face. But I could see the misery and frustration in her eyes so I just said something about needing to do my chores and turned for home, waving goodby as I left.

I still didn't know the truth for sure. But I was beginning to have a pretty good idea.

I got to stay out later than usual for the wiener roast because my brothers were there, too. In fact, Don drove our truck. We ended up with three truckloads of kids from junior high through high school ages. It was lots of fun, but all evening I couldn't get a nagging thought out of my mind.

When I got into bed later, I let my thoughts run their course. I was beginning to see that trouble can come in any form from any direction. And it can come when you least expect it. The end result of my thinking was that whether or not the rumors about Daisy were true, none of it was anybody's business. Not mine. Not anybody's. I'll just have to keep on being Ivy's friend and wait while her family works things out in their own way. I fell asleep with that thought.

We've been studying poetry for the past month in Miss Freeman's class and I was beginning. to comprehend some of the poems I had read earlier and wondered about.

"Today class, I want you to turn to page 127. Look at Emily Dickinson's poem, 'I Died for Beauty.' Now follow along in your books as I read it."

Her voice flowed over and around us and the words took on new meaning. She didn't just read the words, she felt them and gave them life. And those feelings passed into us as we followed along.

"He questioned softly 'Why I failed?'
'For beauty,' I replied—
'And I—for Truth—Themself are One—
'We Brethren, are,' He said—"

Is that right? Are truth and beauty parts of a larger whole? Is one necessary to the other? I have to think about that. I've been taught that truth is essential in our lives and that integrity and honor are integral parts of truth.

But beauty? I thought beauty was something entirely different. I can't remember ever hearing the two connected in any of my Sunday School lessons.

It's true mama loves beauty and has always tried to teach me to understand and appreciate it. But I've always thought beauty involves art and music and literature and sunrises and sunsets and new fallen snow and our sagebrush and piñon-pine tree covered mountains. I had never thought about beauty going beyond things like that. As we continued to discuss the poem, my wonderment increased.

Saturday I hurried through my chores so I could get to the swimming pool as early as possible. By the time I got there, most of the kids in town were already swimming and splashing and water-fighting all over the place. I jumped in and the coolness of the water surprised me. With the day so hot I thought the creek would be warmer.

Someone shouted, "Hey, look who's here!"

I was astonished to see Ivy standing near the dam. She looked uncertain.

"Come on in, Ivy," I yelled, trying for our old camaraderie. "The water's kinda cold but you'll get used to it."

"Yeah, Ivy," I was glad to hear Robbie call, "you won't even notice it in a minute." This seemed to open the gates, and others began calling for her to jump in.

She looked relieved and a lot like her old self as she jumped into the pool. I was pleased. Maybe the old Ivy is finally back.

As it got close to supper time most of the kids started for home. Wanting to talk to Ivy for a minute, I called to Bruce, "Tell mama I'll be there in a few minutes." He nodded and was on his way.

"Are you going to the graduation dance? Mama says that since Bruce is graduating from Ninth Grade I can stay till she and daddy go home."

"Yes," Ivy answered. "Daddy had a good talk with mama and me last night. He said we both have to get on with our lives and quit worrying about what people are saying." Then she added, "Thanks, Emma, for not saying mean things about Daisy. Mama says your mother has been nicer to her than any of the women in the Ladies Hospitality since Daisy left. I think we're all learning something from this. At least I hope so."

"Ivy, are you ready to go?" Robbie stood on the bank

waiting. I was glad he was saving me from having to talk about it any more. It was still a touchy subject for me and I wasn't entirely comfortable with it yet.

"You go on, Ivy. I'm going to take a couple more laps across the pool then I'm going, too." I didn't want to walk back to town with them. They didn't look like they were going to miss me, anyway.

Once across. Good. But I still need to keep my face in the water more. Bruce told me if I put my face into the water and exhale with one stroke then lift it out for a breath with the next, I would improve my speed. And that's what I need to do.

Pushing away from the side, I started across again. As I reached the middle of the pool, I lifted my face out of the water and exhaled and put my face down in the water and started to inhale before I realized I was doing it backwards. With a mouth and nose full of water I coughed and sputtered and thrashed around, throwing water in every direction. I turned toward the dam, spitting muddy water and trying to clear the water out of my eyes so I could see where I was going when a hand grabbed my arm and started pulling me along.

I tried to push the hand away and say that I didn't need any help, I'm doing just fine by myself, when a familiar voice ordered, "For crying out loud, Emma! Stop fighting me! I'm trying to help you get over to the dam so you can get out!"

I gave in and accepted his help, still coughing and sputtering. Reaching the dam, I held onto the gunnysacks on top while I worked to clear out my nose and throat.

"Are you okay now?"

I looked at Jerry blankly. Then it dawned on me. He had never been to the swimming pool. He wasn't there when we built it and when I asked him why he never came swimming, he said something about not being able to.

"I thought you couldn't swim." My breathing was finally back to normal. "What are you doing here?"

"Oh, I climb the mountain over there sometimes and watch you guys fool around in the pool. I was still there just now when you got in trouble."

"I wasn't in trouble! I just breathed at the wrong time and got a mouthful of water." Then I added quietly, "Thanks for coming. to help, though."

"You know, Em, it was pretty stupid of you to swim here alone. You could have been in serious trouble."

"I know," I mumbled, "but that's the only time anybody has room to practice. It's always too crowded." It sounded lame, even to me.

"Why don't you quit kidding yourself. You don't want anybody to see you trying to learn to swim better, do you."

It was a statement and didn't need an answer. But some of the old defiance was still there. "Well, I don't notice you coming to swim when the rest of us are here. When did you learn to swim, anyway?"

He smiled. "I learned when I was ten. I stayed with my grandparents that summer and there was a pond on their farm. Grandma and grandpa let me go out and paddle around in that pond until I could swim across and back." He looked sad. "A train hit grandpa's truck when they were coming home from a meeting one night. I had to go back home right after the funeral."

We rested there awhile longer then he asked, "Are you ready to get out now?"

I nodded. He turned to boost himself up on the dam and I gasped. He turned quickly around.

"My gosh, Jerry, what happened to your back?"

He looked down at his bare chest, confused. "Oh. I forgot I ripped off my shirt when I thought you were in trouble and dove in to help." He reached his hand down to help me climb out. "It's nothing. Just forget about it."

"No, it's not nothing. I promised I wouldn't ask any questions and I won't. But your back looks terrible. I've never seen anything like it. I don't think I'll be able to just forget about it."

I looked steadily at him then stepped around him and walked toward the bank. When we got there he picked up his shirt and put it back on. I noticed some of the buttons were torn off and began to look around in the dirt for them.

Without looking at me, he said so quietly I could hardly hear, "My dad and mom like to drink. And they're drunk nearly all the time. For as long as I can remember they hit and kicked me when they were drinking. Sometimes they burned me with their cigarettes. When I was little I thought it was my fault. But nothing I could do pleased them. A couple of years ago I had a teacher who spent a lot of time talking with me at recess and noon. She helped me see that I wasn't to blame. She arranged with my grandparents for me to stay with them. But after they died I had to go back home. Then last year I nearly died. The doctors at the hospital talked to somebody and that's when Uncle Jim and Aunt Emily were given custody of me."

He paused for a long time. "That's why I never talk about growing up. I want to forget that part of my life. I still don't forgive my mom and dad but I'm trying to learn to understand them. I'll tell you something else I've learned. I will never hit anybody." As we turned to go he added, "Now you know why I don't go swimming."

We walked toward town without speaking. I was still horrified by the mass of scars and welts I'd seen on his back. I wanted to yell and scream and hit somebody for what had been done to Jerry. He sensed my turmoil and let me sort through my thoughts without a word.

We were just coming into town when I stopped and turned to face him. "I can't believe any parent could do what your parents did to you. That's something I've never even thought about. Spankings, yes. I can understand that. I've had a few of those myself. And I've seen some parents shake and jerk their kids around. But I never imagined anything as awful as you've told me. You'll have to give me time to figure this all out. Right now I despise your mom and dad—and I've never even seen them."

Jerry smiled sadly. "You feel like that because you're shocked. I guess part of the reason I didn't want you to know is that I'm ashamed of my mom and dad. But another part is that I knew you'd be upset and angry. But things are different now, Em, and the time will come when you'll get your mind on other things again. That's what my aunt and uncle are helping me do. And it's working. Give it time. You'll see."

I wondered if I would ever really see. I had lots to think about and work through.

Usually when I'm late for supper I have to do the dishes alone. But this time mama knew the minute I walked in the door that something terrible was on my mind. She didn't say anything, just looked at me for a long time.

Later, when daddy and the boys went out to milk the cows I told her about Jerry's back and his explanation.

"I'd heard some of that, Emma, but hoped it was exaggerated. I'm sorry about Jerry and sorry you had to learn about such things. But that, too, is part of growing up. There are vicious people in this world who do wicked things. We just have to be sure we never become like them."

"Is that what Miss Freeman's husband did to her? Did he hurt her as bad a Jerry's mom and dad hurt him?"

"I think so. Rebecca doesn't say much, but I do know that she was in a hospital at least twice."

"But why doesn't somebody help people like that?"

"It's not something people want to recognize. There are those who do try to help, like that teacher Jerry had, but most people still turn a blind eye and a deaf ear. That way they don't have to acknowledge that things like that are going on."

Mama put her arm around me. "Just remember, Mr. and Mrs. Harris stepped in when they found out what was happening to Jerry. And that's why he's here now. And Rebecca did finally get the courage to leave Mr. Bond. And we'll do what we can to help her. So some of us are trying to help. Maybe some day things like this will be brought out into the open and abusers won't be able to get away with such cruelty any more."

"I hope so, mama. When I grow up I'm going to do everything I can to help people like Jerry and Miss Freeman."

And I will, too. I don't know what, but I'll do something.

Chapter Eight

I could hear the uproar long before it reached my house. I knew what it was. We were going to shivaree Mr. Lewis and Miss Conley who just got married. They must be back from Manti. I grabbed a lid and mama's big wooden spoon and rushed out to join the crowd of kids.

We headed for the little house behind the school where the newlyweds would live. Some of us had helped them clean and kalsomine the house and carry in the pieces of furniture people had given them. I had shellacked our old chest of drawers that Mr. Lewis had nailed back together.

The din continued as we worked our way up the street, getting noisier and noisier as more kids ran out from houses along the way. We had all brought pots, pans, cans, lids, spoons, sticks and anything else we could grab to bang together.

When we reached their house, the new Mr. and Mrs. Lewis stood out on their front porch, grinning from ear to ear. They had heard us coming. We banged our utensils louder and louder until Mr. Lewis finally reached into the sack he was holding and began throwing candy kisses into the air. The racket stopped immediately as we scrambled to grab as many kisses as we could.

Shivareeing is such fun. I love it when people get married. We kids always look forward to not only the treats, but the excitement of being part of the wedding celebration.

We already knew the two teachers had waited to get married until school was nearly out so the new Mrs. Lewis could finish teaching. Women don't usually keep teaching once they get married, at least in our area. The Lewises would keep living here in Grassville, however, and next year Mr. Lewis would be back teaching science again. And I'm glad. From what I hear from the kids in his class, he's a much more interesting teacher than I thought he'd be when I first saw him. I look forward to being in his class next year.

After the shivaree we all wandered back home eating candy and kidding around along the way. In a few years some of us will be too old to join the shivarees. So I want to have as much fun with the kids as possible while I still can.

I hurried through my chores before getting ready for the wedding party tonight in the church. They couldn't hold the reception in the school gym, where they're usually held, because it's being decorated for the graduation exercises and dance in a couple of weeks.

I'm really happy about getting to stay for the whole wedding dance. The piano player is sick and Mr. Wilson, the school band teacher, asked me to fill in for her. I've been kinda nervous but have practiced *Deep Purple* and *Whispering* and *Five Foot Two* and *Darkness on the Delta* and all the other songs the orchestra usually plays at the dances, so I'm pretty sure I can do it all right. Mr. Wilson plays the trumpet, my brother Ted plays the drums, Dr. Louganis plays the saxophone and Mr. Ruiz plays the guitar. They teased me during our practices but I knew it was all good-natured fun and teased them back sometimes.

As it got close to midnight I was glad the reception was winding up. I was getting sleepy and knew it would be really hard to keep my eyes open in Sunday School tomorrow morning. Our Sunday School teacher this year is soooo boring! He never reads the lesson until we get in class and then he just keeps his eyes in the manual the whole time as he reads the words in his slow monotone. Most of the time we giggle and whisper, but he goes right on as if he doesn't know we're there. The only thing we're really learning is that in good weather if we get loud enough, he'll stop and say, "Do you want to go outside for the rest of the lesson?"

Of course we always do because once outside, he doesn't even pretend to hold class any longer. He just lets us play games. Now that's when class is interesting!

"Time's up! Pass your papers forward."

As I took the test papers from the person behind me I noticed Joe's name on the top one. As I added mine to the pile I couldn't help noticing that he'd only answered a half dozen questions. Quickly I put my paper on top hoping the teacher wouldn't notice. But he did. I watched as he shuffled through them with a determined look on his face.

His head popped up and he said, "Well Joe, still spending your time whittling instead of studying, huh? You knew the test was today. Why didn't you study for it?"

"I did Mr. Stoker. I just can't remember that stuff." Joe sat on the back row, a head taller than anybody else in class. This was the third year he'd repeated seventh grade. He'd been retained a couple of years in grade school, too.

Most of us kids have known Joe all our lives and we know he'll never be able to memorize all the state capitals. But this is only Mr. Stoker's second year here and I believe he's still convinced he can stuff knowledge into Joe's head if he tries hard enough. He's not really a bad teacher. He just doesn't understand kids like Joe. Hardly any of his teachers have.

Joe Hoffstein's mother died when Joe was ten years old. His father has done his best to try and raise Joe and his little brother alone but with him working. ten hours a day, most of the housework and tending little Billy has been left to Joe. And he does a good job around the house. But school work has always been another matter.

Joe is nearly as old as my brother, Don. He has learned to read easy words and can do simple arithmetic problems. But memorizing long lists of names and places and figuring out how to pass tests are beyond him.

Over the years teachers have tried to work with him. But they haven't known how to change him so year by slow year Joe has been passed from one grade to the next.

After supper, when our chores are finished, most of us kids in town meet at the tennis court. Those of us who have tennis racquets and balls share with the kids who don't. And we all wait in line for our turn to play the winner. Joe is really good at tennis so I'm always glad when we play doubles and I get to be his partner. I'm only fair but I do love to play.

"It looks like we'll be up next, Emma. Think we can beat 'em?"

"Yeah, Joe. I do." I didn't know quite how to bring up what was on my mind so I just blurted it out. "Do you want me to help you try to learn the capitals, Joe? Mr. Stoker's giving everybody one more chance to pass geography."

"Nah. But thanks anyway, Emma. I'll never be able to remember all those towns." He smiled ruefully. "But it don't matter anyway."

"What do you mean?"

"It don't matter whether I pass or not. I'm about finished with school."

"Sure. We all are after next week."

"No, that's not what I mean. I'm not going back to school any more after this year."

"But Joe, you have to go to school. It's the law."

He grinned, "The law just says we have to go to school till we're eighteen. I'll be eighteen in August."

"But what'll you do if you don't go to school?"

"I'll work in the sawmill. Mr. Kenner already promised me a job there full time. I've been workin' there every summer since I was fifteen. I love workin' with wood." I thought about all the beautiful carved figures Joe has made over the years. "Yes. That makes sense for you to work at the mill. What does your dad say about you quitting school?"

Joe laughed, "He don't care. He didn't go past the eighth grade himself. And he knows I've never been very good at all that school stuff." He looked across the court at his brother waiting with the kids on that side. "But we're both real proud of Billy. He's goin' to end up with enough schoolin' for both of us."

I thought about Billy. He was two years younger than me and had already had one double promotion. "Yeah, he's really smart all right." I tapped Joe on the arm with my racquet. "But he'll never be as good looking as you are."

Joe's laugh filled the warm evening air. "Emma, you are somethin' else. Come on," he pulled me to my feet, "it's our turn. Let's knock the socks off those two."

I grabbed the dishtowel and started drying the dishes as fast as Bruce could wash them. It was already past two o'clock and we knew most of the kids would be in the pool by now.

"Slow down, you two. I know you're in a hurry to go swimming, but I don't want you putting dirty dishes in the cupboard."

"We won't, mom," Bruce said as he winked at me, "you know it's a poor dish wiper who can't wipe the dishes clean."

I flipped him with the dishtowel while we all three laughed at the tired old joke. I watched mama as she put the loaves of bread in the oven. I knew she was a teacher before she got married. "Mama, did you ever teach any kids like Joe Hoffstein?"

Mama looked thoughtful. "Just one, my second year teaching."

"Did he learn anything?"

"She. My student was a girl. And yes, she learned to read and write and do easy addition and subtraction. Why?"

"Yeah, Em, why are you asking about that?" Bruce flipped water on me, "And why aren't you keeping up with me?"

Grabbing another dish I answered, "I played tennis with Joe the other day. He says he's going to quit school when this year is over."

"I don't blame him," said Bruce. "He's practically grown up and just as well do something besides sit in school any longer."

"Yeah. That's what he said." I turned to mama, "Is that

how Sally Oliver was? Did she have a hard time in school?"

Mama paused. "I think so. She was still in school when we first moved here, but she didn't finish."

I wanted to get my next words right. "Well, I think Joe's really nice..."

"So do I," interrupted Bruce.

"But I don't get it," I continued, putting the last dish away, "why doesn't Joe care that school is so hard for him? He just accepts it."

"Well," Bruce said, "what good would it do if he didn't accept it? He can't change it. And besides, he's a really good guy and makes great things with his hands."

"That's true," mama said, "he's done a fine job helping his father at home and he really is clever with his hands. That's what we all should do—the best we can with the talents we have."

"I just wish teachers knew how to teach kids like him," I said as Bruce and I headed out the door. "I wish there was some special training teachers could get so they'd know how to help kids like Joe instead of trying to embarrass and ridicule them."

There weren't as many kids at the swimming pool as I thought there'd be. Ivy and Robbie were splashing water on each other and Billy and Joe were racing. each other across the pool and back. A few other kids were there, too, some swimming and some sitting on top of the dam. I looked closer at one of the swimmers.

"Hey, Mary! Glad you made it."

She swam to the edge. "I can't stay long but mama said she'd be okay for a little while. Come on in. The water's warm."

Bruce and I both jumped in. He swam across fast while I visited with Mary.

"Can you believe we've only got one more week of school?"

"I know. The year's gone really fast." I paused, not sure whether I was being too nosy or not. Finally, I asked quietly, "Will you guys have to move again?"

Mary smiled happily, "No. Mr. Kenner gave dad a steady job at the mill. And he says we can move up into that house behind the mill office. We're all really glad."

"So am I. Maybe you can come to the tennis court sometimes. Can you play tennis?"

"I've never tried."

"That's okay. I'm not very good but I'll teach you if you want."

"Sounds good. I'm pretty sure I'll be able to get away sometimes now that the kids are getting bigger and mama's getting stronger." She grinned and said, "Come on, I'll race you across the pool."

We swam together for a while longer then Mary said she

had to go home. She picked up her towel and waved as she left.

"Looks like you and Mary are getting to be good friends." Ivy sounded wistful, "Do you like her?"

"Yeah. She's neat. And you'd like her, too, if you got to know her." I looked around. "Where'd Robbie go?"

"He's over there talking to Bruce. They're going to have a diving contest."

I looked at the two of them poised on the top of the dam. "What's the deal?"

"They're betting on who can stay under the longest."

"I don't think that's a good idea. It's hard to see anything under the water." I turned to yell at them to knock it off just as the two dove in.

We all watched as a few bubbles rose to the surface. It seemed like forever before Robbie's head re-appeared. He started to call, "I won..." when he realized Bruce was still under. "Rats!" he said, "I thought sure I beat him."

I swam over to where they'd dived in. "Something's wrong," I screamed in panic. "Nobody can hold their breath this long!"

Before I could get another word out, Joe dove cleanly into the pool. In a split second he was back up, dragging a limp Bruce with him. Blood and water flowed freely down Bruce's face.

"Give me a hand!" Joe yelled. Instantly Billy and Robbie

helped lift Bruce out of the water. Joe carried him to his pickup truck and laid him carefully in the back. Billy climbed in beside Bruce, pressing a towel to his forehead.

Running as fast as I could, I scrambled into the back with Billy and Bruce as Joe started the engine.

Before we got to the doctor's office, Bruce opened his eyes and looked around wildly.

"It's okay," Billy said calmly. "You cut your head."

"How?" Bruce asked thickly.

Brushing away my tears I told him about diving with Robbie. Then his eyes cleared and understanding returned.

"Yeah. I remember now. I tried to dive deep so I'd stay down longer. But my head bumped on something. I can't remember anything else."

"You must have knocked yourself out," said Billy. "But don't worry, here's the doctor's office."

Joe insisted on carrying Bruce in while Bruce kept insisting he could walk. Billy and I trailed along behind them.

Joe, Billy and I waited in the waiting room until Dr. Louganis came out. "Bruce will be okay. I had to take a few stitches but the cut is right at his hair line so there won't be much of a scar. He's lucky he's not any heavier or he'd have hit that boulder much harder."

He sighed. "You kids take some dumb chances at that pool sometimes." Then he smiled, "But I can't blame you. I used to do the same things when I was your age.

He looked at me, "Just tell your mother to have Bruce

stay quiet the rest of the day. He'll have a headache tomorrow but he's young and he'll heal fast. Head wounds always bleed a lot but they're usually not as bad as they look."

I didn't mind doing the dishes alone after supper while Bruce rested. I'm just glad he's not hurt worse. Bruce looked at me and said quietly, "The doctor said I can't go swimming until my cut is all better."

He winced as he turned toward mama. "I know you've warned us about diving in the pool. I'll remember next time. And I won't get suckered into any more 'chicken' bets, either."

Chapter Nine

The last week of school was a whirlwind of handing in final papers, taking tests and cleaning out our desks. After school every day we met at the swimming pool or the tennis court. We teased each other about getting promoted or being held back. I can hardly believe I'll be in the eighth grade next year. This has been a great school year and I've learned so many new things.

Thursday would be our last English class. When we come tomorrow it'll be just to get our report cards and pick up our corrected papers. Then we'll all help clean the school and get ready for the graduation exercises at night.

Before we handed in our books, Miss Freeman asked us to turn to the Elinor Wylie poem called 'Nonsense Rhyme' and read it aloud together.

> Whatever's good or bad or both
> Is surely better than the none;
> There's grace in either love or loathe;
> Sunlight, or freckles on the sun.
>
> The worst and best are both inclined
> To snap like vixens at the truth;

But, O, beware the middle mind
That purrs and never shows a tooth!

Beware the smooth ambiguous smile
That never pulls the lips apart;
Salt of pure and pepper of vile
Must season the extremer heart.

A pinch of fair, a pinch of foul,
And bad and good make best of all;
Beware the moderated soul
That climbs no fractional inch to fall.

Reason's a rabbit in a hutch,
And ecstasy's a were-wolf ghost;
But, O, beware the nothing much
And welcome madness and the most!

"Now class, think about what we've read. You have learned that each poem speaks to each individual so, consequently, there are no wrong interpretations. I know you know this from the papers you have handed in this week. So now, explain what this poem says to you."

She waited while we pondered. Finally, one or two hands slowly raised. As Miss Freeman called on each one, the responses included the intertwining of both good and bad in the world and that most of us have some of each within us.

She listened and nodded and asked for clarification occasionally but seemed to be waiting for something more.

Then Jerry raised his hand...a first for him. "I think it's more than there being good or bad. That's obvious. And I agree that each of us has some of both, too. But I think the poem goes beyond that. Doesn't it say something in the bible about being neither hot or cold?"

"Yes," murmured Miss Freeman, "The quote is from Revelation and says, 'So then because thou art lukewarm, and neither cold nor hot, I will spue thee out of my mouth.' But go on. Explain what you mean."

"Well, the lines, 'Whatever's good or bad or both Is surely better than the none;' says basically the same thing. Then when it talks about the worst and best both inclined to snap like vixens at the truth, 'But, O, beware the moderated soul That climbs no fractional inch to fail,' and again," Jerry continued to read, "'But, O, beware the nothing-much' all say to me that we have to take a stand on important issues."

He looked intently at Miss Freeman, then glanced around the room, "We may be right or we may be wrong, but to feel nothing and do nothing, I think, is the worst wrong of all." He hesitated, then lowered his eyes and sat down. But no one mocked his explanation. We were too busy thinking about his conclusions.

"Could that be right, Miss Freeman?" Mary asked

thoughtfully. "Is it worse not to take a stand on something? To choose to remain indifferent, and not get involved?"

Mary had put into words what I was thinking. Could sitting on the fence be worse than falling in the mud?

"Yeah, but sometimes deciding one way or the other is hard. What if we make a wrong choice? What happens then?" asked Nick.

"Then we have to accept the consequences and try to learn from them," Jerry answered. "But, at least, we won't be like 'the middle mind that purrs and never shows a tooth!' We won't be 'neither cold nor hot.'"

"Yes," Miss Freeman said, "I believe that's what this poem wants us to think about. We're all faced with choices. And some of them are very hard." She paused and I thought of the hard choice she had made. "Each one of us has to decide which way to go, what choices to make."

Memories of my talk with mama after my run-in with Mr. Bond surfaced. "I think that's true. My mother and I talked about choices." Miss Freeman gave a slight nod. "Mama told me there would be times when I would have to make some hard decisions. She said others will try to help, but in the end the choice will have to be my own."

"She is right," Miss Freeman smiled. "Each of us has to make choices, even young people like you. As you grow up you'll find that sometimes it will seem easier not to make a decision one way or the other. When that happens, think again about the words of this poem and the dangers of the 'middle mind' and the 'nothing much.' Maybe they will help you determine what your choice should be."

She continued, "And now, I've made some choices I'm really pleased with. I have come to know and respect each of you and I have decided to give you something that I hope will help you always remember the importance of words. You have learned this year that Emily Dickinson is one of my favorite poets. She wrote a very little poem with a very big message: 'A word is dead, When it is said, Some say. I say it just Begins to live That day.'"

Her gaze was thoughtful. "With this in mind, I have decided to give each of you one of my books. I have tried to pick out the right book for the right person. I hope you will cherish them as much as I do."

With that, she walked to the closet and lifted out an armful of books. As we each took the book she handed us, I knew she was giving us something very precious. As I watched the expressions on the kids' faces, I was pretty sure they were feeling the same thing.

"You have done some good thinking, not only about this poem, but about other discussions we have had this year. I am pleased with your growth and pleased that I have had the opportunity to be your teacher. I will be gone most of this summer. I'm planning to take some university classes. But if all goes well, I'll see you back here again in the fall."

We all lingered after the bell rang. No one wanted to leave. Miss Freeman's warmth and love wrapped around us in a mantle of comfort and strength. She had given us more than a passing desire to read. She had taken words and given them life and meaning that would enrich us all our lives. And we knew it. Even the kids who had jeered at books the most at the beginning of the school year now carried their books openly and proudly.

The sawmill is the opposite direction from the school and my house but I promised Mary I'd go see their new house. So that's where we headed as soon as school was out.

"This house is much bigger than our other place," Mary told me. I had never been inside any of those little two room 'tag town' houses but I had seen them from the outside and it wasn't hard to imagine what they looked like inside.

I'm not sure what I was expecting, but I was in for a big surprise. When I followed Mary into their new house I noticed that everything was immaculate. The furnishings were sparse but the few things they had were spotless.

Mary's mother was just pulling a pan of cookies out of the oven and the aroma was heavenly. She said warmly, "Welcome to our home, Emma. Would you girls like a cookie while Mary shows you around?"

"I'd love one! They smell delicious! Thanks."

We ate our cookies as I looked around the cheery

kitchen. The window was shining and the curtains framing it were bold reds and yellows. They matched beautifully the red and white checked cloth covering the table. Colorful woven throw rugs lay in front of the sink and the stove. When Mary saw me looking at them she said, "My mother wove them." Then she added shyly, "I made the tablecloth and curtains. I like to help my mother sew."

"They're great," I said, thinking ruefully of the uneven, slipshod dishtowels I'd tried to hem on mama's sewing machine last summer.

We walked through the front room and into her parents' bedroom. A beautiful knitted pastel afghan covered the double bed. "Your mother's work?" I asked.

Mary nodded.

"I suppose you knit, too," I said enviously.

Mary burst out laughing. "I'll make you a deal. You teach me to play tennis and I'll teach you to knit."

"You're on," I grinned.

Then we went into the second bedroom. There were two beds with a colorful chest of drawers between them.

"Where did you get that gorgeous chest of drawers?" I couldn't keep the envy out of my voice.

"My dad made it from scrap lumber Mr. Kenner gave him," Mary replied. "And he painted it the colors of the desert. He says he never wants to forget the beautiful colors in New Mexico where he grew up."

"It's beautiful. Your dad and mother are both artists." Mary nodded in agreement.

On the way home I thought about Mary and her family and the wrong impressions I used to have of the 'tag town' families. It feels good not to be carrying around so many prejudices and misconceptions.

Chapter Ten

Friday at noon we exploded out of the school doors and down the steps like a waterfall cascading over a cliff. Ivy and I chattered excitedly as we walked home together. Talking nonstop we covered everything from school to Robbie to swimming to tennis to Bruce's accident.

When we finally hit a lull in the conversation she said pensively, "I've seen you talking to Mary Ruiz a lot lately. What's she like?"

"She's great," I answered with enthusiasm. "Like I told you at the pool, you'd like her, too, if you got to know her better."

"Maybe." She brightened suddenly, "Maybe I'll invite her to my birthday party. Are you going to invite her to yours?"

I realized that Ivy was working hard to turn over a new leaf. But I also recognized the old Ivy trying to beat the competition. It's strange, but I really don't care about that stuff any more.

"Yes, I'm going to invite her...and some of the other 'tag town' kids, too." I found myself grinning. It feels so good to say what I want to say to Ivy.

And she must feel okay, too, because she nodded and said, "Yeah, me too."

That night we got back up to the school early so we could get a good seat. We weren't the only ones, either. The gym was packed by the time the graduation exercises started. "Bruce looks good in his new suit, doesn't he?" I whispered to mama. He was sitting up on the stage with the other ninth graders. You could hardly see the bandage the way his hair fell over his forehead. It seems funny to think he'll be riding the bus to Sommerset next year and I'll be the only one in our family still going to school here.

I'm so glad I have other friends besides Ivy now. She'll always be my best friend but it won't be any longer because I'm afraid I'll be without friends. That knowledge gives me a lot more confidence in myself.

I glanced over to the side of the stage where the teachers were sitting. Miss Freeman sat there so calm and serene no one would ever guess the terrible things that have happened to her. I remember vividly her telling me that I remind her of herself when she was my age. My goal is to be like she is when I'm her age. With a start of guilt I realized that she had caught me staring at her. Giving me a quick wink and a broad smile, she turned her attention back to the speaker. So did I.

"Do you want to dance?"

My mind flickered back to the night of the Deer Hunt Dance. I smiled at the reflection of my previous insecurities.

As we danced, Jerry talked about his plans for the summer. Mr. Greeley had hired him to be the stock boy and janitor at the store and confectionery. He was really pleased about that.

"But that won't give you any time to play tennis or..." I felt my face flush. Here I am again running my mouth before my brain is in gear.

He laughed. "Hey, don't be embarrassed. It's true I won't go swimming when other kids are around. But maybe we can sneak up there sometimes real early in the morning before anybody shows up."

I'd like that.

"And maybe," he continued, "some days we can get in a game of tennis before I go to work, too."

"You've thought of everything, haven't you," I laughed. "Okay. I hate to get up early, but maybe it'll be fun once in awhile."

As the dance stopped for intermission, we heard the sound of distant thunder. Someone said, "It's kinda early for thunderstorms, isn't it?"

"It is a little early," daddy answered. "But it's been so hot, I'm not surprised. When we get hot weather this early in the year, we seem to get early thunderstorms, too."

"It sounds like it's coming from up the canyon," Jerry said.

"Could it cause a flood?" I wondered aloud. "I'd sure hate to lose our dam so early in the summer."

"I wouldn't worry about it if I were you," Mr. Harris said, "The storm will probably blow over."

But the weather was soon forgotten as the program began. I hadn't seen Miss Freeman since the graduation exercises. I assumed she was in the band room practicing with the eighth grade choir. She's been their director all year and they're really good. I'm definitely planning to take choir next year if she continues as the director.

The choir didn't disappoint us during the intermission program, either, with their renditions of *The World is Waiting for the Sunrise*, *Battle Hymn of the Republic* and a medley of popular songs. When they finished, they got a standing ovation and were called back to sing two encores.

As the dance began again I saw Miss Freeman say something to mama and then slip out the door. A few minutes later I watched as Freddie Oliver staggered out the door and down the stairs. Poor guy, I thought. I don't believe I've ever seen him sober.

"Let's get some refreshments," Jerry said, "they look good." We worked our way over to the refreshment table where punch and cookies were being served. As we picked up our plates we heard thunder again.

"Let's go outside and see if there's lightening, too." Although I've been warned to stay inside during electric storms, thunder and lightening always fascinate me.

We took our goodies and walked out the front door and

around to the side by the playground. We sat down on the low wall and proceeded to munch away.

"Remember when we came out here after the Christmas program?"

Jerry chuckled. "Yeah. You really surprised me that night."

"I know." I took a drink of punch. "I surprised myself, too."

"Well, I'm sure glad you did that. I really felt bad that I'd hurt your feelings," he said.

Just then a streak of lightening flashed across the sky.

"Oh, wow! Look at that! Let's count and see how far away it is."

We got to nine before thunder sounded. "It's still a ways away, but maybe we'd better go back inside."

"Wait a minute, Jerry. I want to see if it's getting closer or moving away."

When the next streak lighted the night, I didn't think about the thunder. "Jerry! Someone's over there by the corner! I saw something move!" I found myself whispering.

"Where?"

"Right over there by the first grade window."

"I can't see anything. You probably imagined it."

Irritated, I answered, "I didn't either. I saw somebody over there."

Lightening streaked again. Nothing moved but in the

flash of light we could see something on the ground. We both stood and walked cautiously over to the corner of the building. Even through the darkness we could make out a shape lying there.

"It's Miss Freeman," I gasped. "I recognize her dress."

We knelt and looked into her face. Lightening flashed again. We could see blood everywhere. Her eyes were closed but her lips were moving like she was trying to speak.

"Quick, get help! I'll stay here with her."

Jerry turned and ran past the playground and around the corner to the front of the school. I sat down and gently cradled Miss Freeman's head in my lap.

"Miss Freeman, Miss Freeman. Can you hear me?"

Her eyes fluttered open. She whispered something.

"What? I can't hear you." I leaned closer to her. I could see the effort to speak was almost too much for her.

"...don't...sad...light...beauty..." I could only pick out those four words. Then she went limp.

Tears streamed down my face. "Please don't die, Miss Freeman," I begged.

A movement caught my eye. I turned as a dark form scurried away from the shadows of the smokestack.

Lightening flashed again and I looked up into a pair of ominous, ice cold, blue eyes. Just then the front door of the school banged open, the sound echoing through the heavy air.

Mr. Bond leaned close. "Say one word and you're dead!"

With that he sprinted toward the alley behind the school. Before Jerry and the others got to us, I heard a vehicle start and slip quietly down the dark alley.

There is no ambulance in Grassville so Miss Freeman was lifted gently into the backseat of our car, her head and shoulders cradled in mama's arms. I grabbed Jerry's hand and pulled him into the front seat with us and daddy drove off toward Dr. Louganis's office. By this time, the rain was coming down in large drops and lightening and thunder were crashing all around.

Chapter Eleven

Mama and daddy and Jerry's aunt and uncle sat quietly talking in the waiting room as Jerry and I stood silently near the doctor's closed examination room door. Dr. Louganis and his wife had hurried home from the dance ahead of us to get things ready. Mr. and Mrs. Harris had followed us from the schoolhouse in their car.

Please, Heavenly Father, don't let her die, I prayed soundlessly over and over.

Sometimes when I looked up I found Jerry's eyes fastened on my face. He didn't say anything but I knew he was aware of my prayers.

"Do you think she'll die?" I could hardly whisper the words.

Jerry didn't answer for a long time. Finally he said, "There are worse things than dying. You have to learn to accept that."

"I can't accept it and I won't!"

"Do you know who did this to her?" He looked thoughtful as I shook my head, afraid to speak.

Before he could say anything more we heard a low roar, growing rapidly in volume. It sounded like a sustained roll of thunder that wouldn't quit.

"Flood!" We all looked at each other. The sound increased as the flood raced down the creek through town.

"Jim, do you think we should check on the children?" Anxiety made Mrs. Harris's voice quiver.

"They're fine, Emily. Don't worry about them." He patted her hand. "Your mother said she'd stay with them all night if she was needed."

Daddy spoke up, "You don't need to worry about the flood. You can tell by the sound that it's not over the creek banks."

Just then Dr. Louganis stepped into the room. We all looked at him expectantly. "There's still no change. She hasn't regained consciousness."

"Is she going to make it?" Mama's voice broke.

"I can't tell yet. She's suffered severe head and torso trauma. She needs to be in a hospital."

"There's no chance of that tonight, I'm afraid," daddy said. "Listen to that rain. The road will be a sea of mud."

"Yes. I know." He put his hand on the doorknob, "You might as well go on home. Athena and I are doing everything that can be done here."

I looked up sharply. Before I could protest, mama said quietly, "We'd like to stay here awhile longer, Steve. We want to be here if she comes to."

Dr. Louganis nodded. He looked solemn as he turned the knob and walked back into the examination room, shutting the door quietly behind him.

As we listened to the storm outside, another kind of storm raged in me. I knew I should tell what happened, but fear kept the words trapped inside my head.

I jumped as the outer door burst open. Sheriff Watson stepped inside, water pooling around his feet.

"I just got a call from the Junction. The flood just took out the bridge there." Now there was no chance to get to the hospital in Sommerset.

The sheriff looked at Jerry and me. "You two found her, didn't you?"

We nodded.

"Did either of you see anyone else?"

Jerry said, "No," while I stood there with my eyes on the floor.

The sheriff turned to the others, "Everybody I've talked to said Freddie Oliver left just a few minutes after Rebecca did. Did any of you notice that?"

Mama nodded her head, but the others said, "No."

"I didn't even see Rebecca leave," Mrs. Harris said. "Surely you don't think Freddie did this to her?"

Daddy looked incredulous. "Everybody knows he was drunk, but he wouldn't hurt a fly."

"It would seem so. But no one else left around the time she did. Freddie's the only suspect I've got." He added slowly, "It doesn't make sense to me either, but I'm afraid I'll have to lock him up."

I couldn't bear it. I know Freddie didn't do anything. But I also remember Mr. Bond's eyes boring into mine when he told me he'd kill me.

He will, too. Of that I'm sure. This is the first time in my life I've felt such abject terror. Is this how it was for Miss Freeman? How did she live with this kind of fear?

And then I thought of her words to me, "...light...beauty..." What did she mean? That's the first thing I'm going to ask her when she gets better.

Sheriff Watson walked over to the door. He turned as he opened it, "I'll be back before long." He paused. "With this storm there's no good looking for anything to help me around the school. Everything will be washed away." The rain sounded fierce and foreboding beyond the door. I stared after him, wondering what menace waited for me out in that wicked night.

"Come over and sit down." Mama looked at Jerry and me, "You both look exhausted."

That's funny, I thought, as we sank into the chairs, I've never been up this late and I'm not even tired.

All I could think about was Miss Freeman's battered face as it lay in my lap. And the look on Mr. Bond's face as the lightening flashed. With my mind in the midst of a dozen conflicting thoughts, I picked up bits and pieces of the conversation around me.

"...not possible...Freddie Oliver..."

"...drunk...staggering all over the place..."
"...his mother...poor soul..."
"...Rebecca...say anything?"
I realized they were all looking at me. "What?"
"I said didn't Rebecca say anything at all to you, Emma?"
I shook my head. I couldn't look at daddy.
"She's tired," I heard Mrs.Harris whisper.
No! I'm not, I wanted to shout. I'm not tired! I'm scared and mixed-up and don't know what to do!
Jerry looked steadily at me. But the others turned away, murmuring quietly. My thoughts once again piled on top of each other.
You can't let Freddie take the blame for this.
You heard what Mr. Bond said. He'll do the same thing to you as he did to Miss Freeman.
But it's still not right!
Is dying right? Freddie's just an old drunk. He's probably better off locked up anyway.
That's terrible, Emma! You know better than that! You know you do!
Yes, but it's not fair. It's not my fault Mr. Bond hurt Miss Freeman.
No. And it's not Freddie's fault, either!
But Mr. Bond is a horrid, brutal, vicious man and...
"It's getting cold in here." Mama rubbed her arms.

"I'm roasting."

Mama leaned over and put her fingers on my forehead. "Are you coming down with something, Emma? You don't feel hot."

Neither cold nor hot. Where have I heard that? It hasn't been too long ago. And then the words of the poem came tumbling back.

"Whatever's good or bad or both Is surely better than the none;...The worst and best are both inclined To snap like vixens at the truth;...Beware the moderated soul..."

"That climbs no fractional inch to fall," Jerry finished.

I looked at him in surprise. I didn't realize I'd been whispering the lines.

Jerry spoke again, so quietly no one else could hear, "Something's wrong, isn't it? Something more than Miss Freeman being hurt?"

'But, O, beware the nothing-much And welcome madness and the most!' I looked at him. "Yes, something's terribly wrong and..."

Before I could finish, Sheriff Watson quietly opened the door and stepped inside. It was calm outside now, I noticed as he closed the door.

"The flood's pretty well gone down and the storm has passed." He looked around the quiet room, "Miss Freeman?"

We all turned as the examination room door opened. Dr. Louganis stood there shaking his head, his wife behind him quietly weeping.

"No!" I screamed. "She's not dead! She can't be dead!" Mama put her arms around me, not saying a word. But I felt her tears slide down my cheek.

"Well, that's it, then. I'll have to go pick up Freddie." Sheriff Watson turned to open the door.

'And welcome madness and the most!' The words shrieked in my head. "No," I whispered, "Freddie didn't do it."

And then everything came tumbling out without stopping. Between great gulping sobs, I told about Miss Freeman trying to talk, and Mr. Bond coming out of the shadows where he'd been hiding, and what he said to me, and how he looked when he said it, and how his truck went down the alley without lights just about the time Jerry and the others reached us.

"I'm sorry," I said over and over, ashamed. "But I'm so scared I didn't dare say anything."

They looked at me with compassion, tears running down their faces. Even the men. I was surprised. I've never seen a man cry.

Finally the sheriff asked, "You can't mean Tony Bond? The sheriff from over in Sage County? How could you possibly know him? Are you sure you didn't make a mistake?"

"No, I didn't make a mistake. I met him the day before Thanksgiving. He came to school looking for a Mrs. Bond."

"That's right," daddy spoke up, "Rebecca had already told Livvy about him."

"Sheriff Bond?" Sheriff Watson shook his head like he was trying to clear it. "I can't believe it. I've worked with him on a few cases over the years. He's got a good reputation as one of the top officers in law enforcement circles. Why would he do something like this?"

And then mama quietly told Rebecca's story. Everyone was dumbfounded.

"Why didn't she get help before?" I'd almost forgotten Dr. Louganis was there.

"She tried. More than once she tried. But from your surprise, Dick," she looked at Sheriff Watson, "I can see why she couldn't convince anyone."

Miss Freeman was buried in our little cemetery on the east side of town the following Monday. Everyone came to the funeral. The church couldn't hold them all so some had to stand outside and listen through the open door and windows. There wasn't a dry eye in the church or at the cemetery.

My sleep was fitful that night. Conflicting dreams battled for precedence. Sometimes I saw Miss Freeman's shining smile beckoning me to join her. But I couldn't reach her. Then she was lying on the ground with rain beating down on her and flood waters reaching out to engulf her. I tried to help her but Mr. Bond stepped between us, his mouth twisting cruelly as he warned, "I'm going to kill you. I'm going to kill you."

More than once I found myself crying, wrapped in mama's arms while she whispered words of comfort. The sky was changing from black to gray before I finally fell into dreamless sleep.

The next afternoon Sheriff Watson came to our house. "They found Sheriff Bond."

I stiffened. I've been dreading this. The thought of having to face him again sends shivers down my spine. I know, somehow, he'll keep his promise to me.

The sheriff continued, "His body was found at the edge of the creek not far from his truck, two miles below the Junction. It looks like he was on the bridge when it was washed away."

He looked directly at me, "You don't have to be afraid any more."

I nodded, not trusting myself to speak.

"I just don't understand," he went on, "those of us who worked with him thought we knew him. Now we realize we didn't know him at all."

Mama said softly, "I wonder if any of us really know each other. The faces we show the world aren't always the same faces we see in the mirror."

"Or others see reflected there," daddy added.

I understand a little what they mean. In just this year alone I have seen different sides of Ivy and Jerry and Mary and Miss Freeman. And yes, of myself. Is this what life is all about? That needs some serious thought.

Excusing myself, I walked outside and began climbing my mountain. Only there will I find answers.

Chapter Twelve

As they had predicted, summer was hot. The storm, which still haunts my dreams sometimes, ushered in both heat and humidity. The kids in town had repaired and rebuilt the dam for our swimming pool but I don't swim as often as I'd planned. My heart isn't in it yet.

One day at the store I heard Sheriff Watson talking about the flood that killed Mr. Bond. The water out of our canyon had been joined by the water in Coyote and Cougar Canyons so it was overflowing the banks by the time it reached the Junction. "I'm surprised Tony even tried to cross the bridge. He must have thought he could outrun it."

There was a welcome, early evening breeze coming out of the canyon as I worked my way past the gravestones, carrying the bouquet of peonies. Mrs. Oliver had been in her yard as I passed and had asked me if I would mind taking some of her flowers to Rebecca's grave. Everybody called her that now. 'Miss Freeman' was wrong somehow, and we hadn't had the opportunity to know her as Miss O'Brien.

I guess it wasn't hard for Mrs. Oliver to figure out where I was going. I go to the cemetery every week. Mama told me not to worry when I said Ivy thinks I am being morbid.

"She just doesn't understand, Emma. Visiting Rebecca's grave is helping you work through your grief. It's a natural thing. The time will come when you won't need to go so often, when life will settle back into its familiar routine. But it will never be quite the same, either. The hole she left will never fill in. But the sharp edges will soften and become smooth."

I know she still thinks about my six-year old sister who drowned in grandpa's canal the year I was born. Mama doesn't talk about her much but I know she still misses her.

I wonder, I thought as I laid the flowers gently on Rebecca's grave, if the sharp edges will really ever smooth out. It hurts so much to think about what happened to Rebecca. If I only knew what she was trying to tell me, maybe I could find comfort.

I watched as Jerry came walking among the gravestones. He was carrying a bouquet of flowers, too. I recognized them from his aunt's flower garden.

He laid them next to Mrs. Oliver's peonies and we walked over to a nearby tree and sat in companionable silence under its branches, not wanting or needing to speak. I know Jerry misses her as much as I do and I know he knows how much I miss her. Rebecca had changed all our lives. We had known her for such a short time, yet she seemed to have known us forever.

"Do you believe she's happy now?" I needed confirmation.

He waited for a minute then said slowly, "I have to believe that. Otherwise there's no sense to anything at all."

"Yeah," I agreed, glad he was helping me solidify my own feelings. "Have you read the books she gave you?" He had told me Rebecca had given him other books besides the one she gave each of us in class that last day.

"I finished *Gulliver's Travels* the other day and am just getting started on *A Tale of Two Cities*. Isn't it strange how she gave away all her books that last day?"

"Almost like she knew she wouldn't be here for us and wanted to give each of us a part of herself." I picked a blade of grass and began chewing on it. "Did you know she left a note on her dresser leaving her clothes to Sally Oliver?"

"Yes. Aunt Emily said Mrs. Oliver cried when she told her about it."

"I wonder how she knew?" I wiped a tear away and thought about life and death, wondering if I would ever understand it all.

"Do you remember how Max used to laugh whenever he saw someone with a book?"

"How could I forget? He never missed a chance to tease about stuff like that?"

"Well, when I was sweeping the confectionery last night, he came in and asked me if I'd loan him *Call Of The Wild.*"

"Max!? What did you tell him?"

Jerry smiled. "I told him sure. I knew he was a secret reader before school was out. He just made fun of others to keep anybody from guessing the truth about him."

Even Max, I thought in amazement. "I guess Rebecca made a difference to everybody. Not just the kids in our class."

I thought of her smile and her warmth and her gentleness. I remembered how her eyes lit up when we discussed a particularly difficult passage from a lesson and one of us gave a thought-provoking response. She had taught us so much. Not just about literature, but about ourselves as well.

The sun had dipped behind the west mountain before we got to the cemetery. Now we watched as its reflection hit the high clouds and turned them a brilliant pink.

"Have you ever figured out what she was trying to say that night?"

I hadn't until that minute. As the sky flamed above us I thought of Victor Hugo's poem she had read to us in class. "I think she was telling us all not to feel bad. I think she was trying to tell us to take what she had given us and get on with our lives."

Jerry joined me as I murmured Rebecca's last message to us.

"Good night! Good night!
Far flies the light;
But still God's love
Shall flame above,
Making all bright.
Good night! Good night!"